Penguin Modern Stories 2

Edited by Judith Burnley

Penguin Books

Penguin Books Ltd, Harmondsworth,
Middlesex, England
Penguin Books Australia Ltd, Ringwood,
Victoria, Australia

First published in book form in Great Britain
by Penguin Books Ltd 1969
Reprinted 1970

Made and printed in Great Britain by
Cox and Wyman Ltd., London,
Reading and Fakenham
Set in Intertype Baskerville

Contents

Introduction

The second volume of our new quarterly contains eight stories which illustrate the versatility of short stories being written today. From John Updike's acute, suspenseful *The Wait* which has the fluency and dense characterization of a short novel, to the distillation of wit and irony, the blend of bawdy and lyrical in Emanuel Litvinoff's *Life Class,* each story creates its own vivid world. They are published here for the first time in this country.

John Updike

The Wait

'Good-bye?'

'Don't say that word to me, Harry. Please don't say it.' Sally's wrist ached from holding the receiver so long, and now her whole forearm began to tremble. She pinched the receiver between her shoulder and her ear and used her freed hands to button one of Peter's straps; in the last few months he had learned to dress himself, all except for the buttons, and she had hardly found it in her scattered wits to praise him. Poor child, he had been standing there for ten minutes waiting for his mother to get through talking; waiting and listening, waiting and watching with that wary glimmering expression on his face – She began to cry. It came upon her like a gentle fit of retching; with clenched teeth she tried to keep her sobs from carrying into the telephone.

'Hey? Don't.' Harry laughed in embarrassment, faintly and far away. 'It's just good-bye for two days.'

'Don't *say* it, damn you. I don't care what you mean, don't *say* it.' I'm crazy, she thought; I'm a crazy woman and he'll start to hate me. At the thought of his hating her after she had given so much of herself to him, she became indignant. 'If all you can do is laugh at me maybe we should say good-bye for good.'

'Oh, Christ. I'm not laughing at you. I love you. I hate it that I can't be there to comfort you.'

Peter nudged closer, to have the other strap buttoned, and she smelled a Life Saver on his breath. 'Where did you get that candy?' she asked. 'We mustn't eat candy in the morning.'

Harry asked, 'Who's there?'

'Nobody. Just Peter.'

'Bobby gave me,' Peter said, and now that glimmering expression seemed about to resolve into fear. Bobby was an older boy who lived next door.

'You go find Bobby and tell him I want to talk to him. Go, sweetie. Go find Bobby and tell him. Mommy will be off the phone in just a minute.'

'Poor Peter,' Harry said in her ear. 'Don't send him away.'

How could he say this, he who had robbed her of all joy in her children? Yet of course it was just that he *could* say it that enlarged her love so helplessly; he refused to remain fixed in the role of lover as she imagined it should be played. A needless kindness kept shattering his shell. Tears burned her cheeks; she held silent to keep her soaked voice from him. Her abdomen and arms physically ached. God, could he be doing it on purpose?

'Hey? Hi?'

'Hi,' she answered. It was a kind of code they had, for moments when the connexion between them seemed to have broken.

'You O.K.?'

'Yes.'

'You can go to the Garden Club while I'm away, and take the children to the beach, and read Moravia – '

'I'm reading Camus now.'

'You're so intelligent.'

'Won't you miss your plane?'

'Take Peter to the beach, and play with the baby, and lie in the sun, and be nice to Richard . . . '

'I can't. I can't be nice to Richard. You've ruined him for me.'

'I didn't mean to.'

'I know, I know.' Harry's fault as a lover, his cruel fault, was that he acted like a husband. He was always gesturing to protect her; but, in their circumstances, his gestures, ineffectual, merely denied her the dignity of the dangerous role she had decided to play.

'Listen,' he said. 'I love you. I wish you could come to Washington with me. But it can't be. We were very lucky to get away with it once. Richard knows something. Ruth knows.'

'She does?'

'Her glands do.'

'Do what?'

'*Know*. Now don't worry about it. It wouldn't have been so lovely the second time anyway. I'll miss you constantly and won't sleep at all in the bed by myself. The air-conditioner going whoosh, whoosh.'

'You'll miss Ruth too.'

'Not so much.'

'No? Hey. I love you for saying, "Not so much". A real lover would have said, "Not at all".'

He laughed. 'That's what I am. An unreal lover.'

'Then why can't I shut you out? Harry, I *hurt*, physically *hurt*. Even Richard feels sorry for me and gives me sleeping pills from his own prescription.'

'Greater love hath no man than to give sleeping pills from his own prescription.'

'I could call Josie this evening and say I'm in Manhattan and the Saab has broken down. It's been acting funny lately, I know they'd believe me.'

'Oh, sweetie. You're so gallant. It would never swing. They'd find out and he wouldn't let you have the children.'

'I don't want the children, I want you.'

'Don't say that. You love your children very much. Just looking at Peter made you cry.'

'It was you who made me cry.'

'I didn't mean to.'

She didn't know how to answer this; she could never tell him that you were responsible for things you didn't mean to do as well as things you did. He believed in God, and that inhibited her from giving him instruction on anything. Through the kitchen window she saw Peter finding Bobby. Peter had forgotten the message she had given him, and the older boy led him out of sight into the woods.

She asked, 'Will you be at the State Department all afternoon? Could I call you there if I come?'

'Sally, don't come. You'll just crucify yourself for nothing. We'd only be there one night.'

'You'll forget me.'

His laugh shocked her, she had meant this so seriously.

'I don't think in two days I'll forget you.'

'You think a night with me is nothing.'

He paused; she felt in the unreeling seconds that she was being given line. 'No,' he said. 'I think a night with you is almost everything. I'm hoping for a lifetime of them.'

'Hoping's a nice safe thing to do.'

'I don't want to fight with you. I never fight with women. I don't think we should take any risks until we know what we're going to do.'

She sighed. 'You're right. I say to myself, "Harry's right". We mustn't be reckless. There are too many other people involved.'

'Crowds of them. I wish they weren't there. I wish the world was just you and me. Listen. You don't want to come. The airlines are all messed up by this strike at Eastern. Right now I can see six generals and a hundred young salesmen of computer parts in Dacron suits shoving towards Gate 17. My plane must be about to board.' He was in a phone booth at La Guardia. The flight he had planned to take had been full; he had killed the time of delay by calling her. She thought, If he had gone on the right plane he wouldn't have called me; and this casualness, the implied smallness of her place in his life, enlarged him, scooped wider with its insult the aching hollow of her love.

He was waiting for her to laugh or agree, she couldn't remember which. 'I love you so much,' she said limply.

'Hey, how will you explain this on your phone bill? I wouldn't have called collect if I'd known we'd talk so long.'

'Oh, I'll just say – I don't know what I'll say. He never listens to what I say anyway.' Sally sometimes wondered how many of her accusations of her husband were unfair. Her conversation was like a garden gone wild; surprising weeds sprang up in it every day.

'They *are* boarding. Good-bye?'

'Good-bye, darling.'

'I'll call you Wednesday morning.'

'Very good.'

He heard a rebuke in her tone and asked, 'Shall I call you from Washington? Tomorrow morning?'

'No, you'll have things to do. Be busy. Just think of me a little.'

He laughed. 'How could I help but?' He waited, said, 'You're the one,' pecked a little flat kiss into the telephone, and hung up. She replaced the receiver quickly, as if stoppering a bottle from which Harry might escape.

Her hair uncombed, her bathrobe flapping, Sally went outdoors and screeched at the edge of the woods, 'Bo-oys! Bee-each!'

The woods screening the houses of the neighbourhood from one another smelled profoundly of summer, not the usual delicate Connecticut scent of thinned underwood and grass but a rich warm odour of layered leaf mould and mouldering logs – the way vacations had smelled when she was a child from Seattle summering in the Cascades. She went upstairs to change, and this nostalgic ferny fragrance, persisting through the bedroom window, intersected the faintly corrupt tang of salt water on her bathing suit. Sally bundled and pinned her hair. Alone in her bathroom, she conjured up Harry; she gave the air his eyes. In making love his first motion was always to remove her hairpins and in the daily details of her toilet she seemed to bend close to him, sharing with him his careful love of her body.

She telephoned Bobby's mother, who was happy to have her take him to the beach with Peter. Day after day, this woman cheerfully consented, and never offered to reciprocate: she stayed in her house and made sculptures out of driftwood. That was what Sally needed, a hobby. She fixed a thermos of lemonade, collected the boys, and got into the car.

Josie was laboriously pushing the baby carriage, a bag of groceries propped at the baby's feet, up the driveway as Sally and the boys drove down. The Saab had lately developed a reluctance to start, and she parked it pointed downhill and used momentum to turn the engine over. Josie had reached just the steep place in the driveway where Sally let out the clutch. The women could exchange only frightened looks in the precarious moment as the spark ignited and the engine jerked into power. Sally felt that Josie had something to ask her, something about meals or naps, but Josie knew the routine as well as she – better, because she was less distracted, was middle-aged and past love.

Under the June sun, Long Island Sound was a flashing plane reflecting the command *Don't go*. She led her son and his friend well down the beach. Ruth lay in the pack of mothers at the other end. Sally discovered herself crying again; she didn't notice until her cheeks registered the wetness. *Don't go*. Everything agreed on this – the grains of sand, the chorus of particles of light alive on the water, the wary glances of her son, the distant splashes and shouts that sounded, when she lay down and closed her eyes, like the smooth clatter of an ethereal sewing machine. *Don't go, you can't go, you are here*. The unanimity was wonderful. He didn't want her to go, he thought a night with her was nothing, he told her she was crucifying herself, he said it would not be as good as the first time. She grew furious with him. Her breathing felt oppressed under the weight of the sun; a rough touch gouged and abraded the skin of her exposed midriff, and she opened her eyes prepared to scream. Peter had brought her a crab claw, weathered and fragrant.

'Don't go, Mommy,' he pleaded, holding out close to her eyes his tattered dead gift. Her ears must be deceiving her.

'It's lovely, sweetie. Don't put it in your mouth. Now go away and play with Bobby.'

'Bobby hates me.'

'Don't be silly, darling, he likes you very much, he just doesn't know how to show it. Now please go away and let Mommy think.'

Of course she shouldn't go. As Harry said, they had been lucky the first time. Richard had been on one of his trips to Chicago. Harry had waited for her at National Airport and they had taken a taxi into Washington. Their taxi-driver, a solemn coloured man who drove his cab with a proprietorial gentleness, had noticed the quality of their silence and asked if they wanted to go through the park, around the Tidal Basin, to see the cherry trees. Harry told him yes. The trees were in blossom, pink, mauve, salmon, white; tremblingly Harry's fingers kept revolving Richard's wedding ring on her finger.

The hotel lobby was dark-carpeted and full of Southern accents. With a lowering of his eyelashes the desk clerk accepted her as Mrs Conant. Perhaps her face had been too radiant. Their room had white walls and framed flower prints, and looked out on an airshaft. Harry shaved with a brush and soap bowl, which she would not have guessed. She thought all men used electric razors, because Richard did. Nor would she have guessed that the first evening, while she was painting her eyes in the bathroom and he was watching Arnold Palmer sink the winning putt on television, he would fall into a depression, and that for fifteen minutes she would have to hold him on the bed while he stared at the white wall and murmured about pain and sin, before he gathered the courage to button his shirt and put on his coat and take her to a restaurant. In an eye-whipping spring wind they walked block after block on the wide, diagonally intersecting streets, looking for a restaurant. Away from the illuminated monuments and façades, Washington seemed dark and secret, like the rear of a stage set. Limousines swished by with a liquid, lonely sound heard in Manhattan only very late at night. She felt the curse slowly lift from Harry's mind. He became manic, and leap-frogged a parking meter, and in the restaurant, a fancy-priced steakhouse catering to Texans, he impersonated a congressman escorting the Queen of the Minnesota Dairyland. Their waiter, eavesdropping, had expected a huge tip, and been plainly disappointed. Strange, how fondly she remembered the awkwardnesses. In a narrow little gift shop, where Harry had insisted on buying toys to take home to his children, the saleswoman kept turning to her as if she were their mother, tentatively, puzzled by her silence. On the last morning, by the elevator, on their way to breakfast, she had been asked by the head chambermaid if the room might be cleaned, and she had said yes; this woman was the first person to treat her without a flicker of doubt as Harry's wife. When they returned at noon, the venetian blinds had been torn from the window, their bed was stripped and shoved against the bureau, and a slouching Negro was lathering the carpet with a softly screaming machine. Harry and Sally left the hotel in one taxi and took separate planes home and found that the coincidence of their absences had not been noticed. Their momentary marriage sank greener and greener into the past and became irretrievable. No matter what happened, it would never happen again, never happen the same, in all of time. It would be silly – insane – to risk everything and go to him now. For now the venetian blinds of their affair were, if not quite torn off, at least set at a revealing tilt: Josie blushed and stiffly left the kitchen when Harry's usual ten-o'clock call began ringing; Richard sat drinking the evenings away with a thoughtful dent in his upper lip; and the glimmering, watchful expression almost never left Peter's face. Even the baby, who was learning to walk, seemed shy of her and preferred to lean on space. Perhaps this was a hallucination – at times Sally truly feared for her sanity.

She stood up. The Sound, tipped higher, massively restated that it was impossible to go. The perfect seam of water and sky seemed to exclude an immense possibility. Panic struck her. 'Bo-oys,' she called. 'Time to go-o!'

Bobby's body twisted and dropped to the sand in a tantrum. He shouted, 'We just came, you nut!'

'Don't ever call people that,' she told him. 'If you're rude, people won't know what a nice little boy you are.' It was one of Harry's theories that if you often enough told someone he was nice he would become nice. In a way, it did work. Peter came to her, and Bobby, afraid of being left alone, sulkily followed to the Saab.

Don't go. No. Yet the command had no weight, no weight whatsoever, and though she read it in a dozen obstructive omens that bristled about her as she dressed and lied her way out of the house and drove to the airport and paid her way on to the aeroplane, it remained a weightless sentence, afloat on the deep certainty that she should go, that going was the only possible thing to do, and absolutely right. A righteous tide lifted her over the snag of Josie's surprise, carried her past the children's upturned faces, pushed her through the choked hurry of dressing and the ominous clogging of the Saab's starter, urged her down the swerving allées of the Merritt Parkway, and sustained her nerve during the wait at La Guardia while United found her a seat on a Washington flight. Then Sally flew; she became a bird, a heroine. She took the sky on her back, levelled out on the cloudless prairie above the clouds – boiling, radiant, motionless – and held her breath for twenty pages of Camus while the air-conditioner nozzle whispered into her hair. The plane canted above a continent of loamy farms where dot-like horses galloped. Acres of small white houses in curved rows swung into view, and then a city composed of diagonal avenues and miniature monuments. Washington's shaft was momentarily aligned down a breadth of Mall with the Capitol dome. The plane skimmed water, thumped, reversed its engines, shuddered, and with a stately swaying waddled to a stop. A departed shower had left the runway damp in patches. The afternoon sun struck from the cement a warmth faintly more tropical than the warmth she had left on the beach. It was three o'clock. Within the terminal, people were rapidly threading their way through the thick aroma of floor wax and hot dogs. She found an empty phone booth. Her hand fumbled inserting its dime, and the quick of her index fingernail hurt as she dialled the necessary numerals.

Harry was a designer and animator of television commercials, and the State Department had hired his company to create a series of thirty-second spots plugging freedom in under-developed countries, and he was the intermediary for the project. From their first trip Sally knew the section of the State Department that could find him. 'He's not a regular employee,' she explained. 'He's just in town for two days.'

'We've found him, Miss. Who shall I say is calling, please?'

'Sally Mathias.'

'Miss Sally Mathias, Mr Conant.'

Some electric noises shuffled. His voice laughed harshly. 'Hi there, you crazy Miss Mathias.'

'Am I crazy? I think I am. Sometimes I look at myself and think, very calmly, You nut.'

'Where are you, at home?'

'Sweetie, can't you tell? I'm here. I'm at the airport.'

'My God, you really did come, didn't you? You're dauntless.'

'You're mad at me.'

He laughed, postponing reassuring her. And when he spoke, it was all in questions. 'How can I be mad at you when I love you? What are your plans?'

'Should I have some? I'll do whatever you want me to. Do you want me to go back?'

She felt him calculating. She saw a Puerto Rican child Peter's age standing apparently abandoned on the waxed floor outside the phone booth. The child's eyes rolled, his little pointed chin buckled, he began to cry. Rigidly Sally restrained a threatened collapse within her. 'Can you kill some time?' Harry asked at last. 'I'll call the hotel and say my wife has decided to come down with me. Take a taxi in, go to the Smithsonian or something for a couple of hours, and I'll meet you along Fourteenth Street, at New York Avenue, around five-thirty.' The door of the booth beside Sally's opened, and a short dark man angrily led the child away.

'Suppose we miss each other.'

'Listen. I'd know you in Hell.' It frightened her that when he said 'Hell' he meant a definite place, which he could half imagine. 'If you feel lost, go into Lafayette Square – you know, the park behind the White House. Stand under the horse's front hoofs.'

'Hey? Harry? Don't hate me.'

'Oh, God. Wouldn't it be nice if I could? Just tell me what you're wearing.'

'The black linen suit.'

'The one you wore at Henrietta's party? Great. There are some terrific trains on the ground floor. Don't miss Lindbergh's plane. See you five-thirtyish.'

'Harry? I love you.'

'Love you.'

He thinks it would be nice to hate me, she thought, and went out and caught a taxi. The driver asked her which Smithsonian she wanted, the old or the new, and she said the old. But at the door the brownstone castle's air of cluttered eternity repelled her, and she instead walked across the Mall in the sunshine, to relish the simple present. The subsiding afternoon, the pavement dappled with shadows and seeds, the popsicle hawkers, the brown-windowed tourist buses stuffed with glaring people, the bunched flocks of children being led by teachers that also seemed children, the fairy ring of fluttering American flags planted around the base of the great obelisk, the little Indian women wearing saris and Brahmin dots and nostril pearls and carrying aqua parasols and briefcases were to Sally all fragments of a fair. In the distance the Capitol dome, cleaner than its grey wings, had the glazed lustre of a piece of marzipan. The sunshine, imprinted everywhere with official images, seemed money to her as she walked past the Natural History Building, up Twelfth Street, through the dank arcades of the Post Office Department, along Pennsylvania Avenue to the fence of the White House. She felt airy, free. The federal buildings, fantastically carved and frosted, floated around her walk; their unreality and grandeur permeated her mood. She looked in at the White House – in the gaps between guards and greenery – and crossed the street.

Sally carried a toothbrush in her pocketbook, and that was her luggage; she had inherited from her father, a travelling china salesman, a love of travelling light. Free, cool in her black linen, she felt like an elegant young widow returning from her husband's spring funeral; he had been an old man, greedy and unkind. In truth, Richard, though heavier than ten years ago, was still handsome enough, though his quick gestures had been slowed and blurred by what he called, with a peppery, resentful intonation, his 'responsibilities'. When their marriage was young, they had lived in Manhattan, and in their poverty had walked miles as amusement. She felt Richard's ghost at her shoulder, remembered the novel rhythm of walking with, of *having,* a man. She had hated schools, prim places of Eastern exile. Richard had rescued her from Barnard and made her a woman; where had it gone, her gratitude? Was she wicked? She couldn't believe it, feeling still so full of sky from the aeroplane ride, sidewalk mica glinting under her, her nostrils pricked by the spicelike odour of tar. The crosswalk stripes had been tugged and displaced by the melting summer heat. On the wide pavements her stride kept overtaking the saunter of Southerners. Church chimes, the chimes of lemon-yellow St John's, sounded the hour. It was five. She walked west along I Street to kill time. Government clerks in flapping lightweight suits squinted through her, towards the distant wife and Martini. A multitude of women had been released.

Like an unbearable golden ornament the sun rode the glassy buildings on her left, and its heavy rays carved her face into self-awareness. She realized she was pouting as she searched the faces for Harry's face.

How he would grin! Despite his scruples and premonition he would grin to see her; he always did, and she alone could bring out that smile in him. Though only a few months older than she, and remarkably innocent for a man of thirty-one, he made her feel like a daughter whose every defiance testified to a cherished vitality. She felt carved on her face a deep smile answering his imagined one.

Danger flicked from the hatted faces. She seemed to see a man she knew, rounding the corner of the BOAC building, across from Farragut's gesturing statue – a young Wall Street scion Richard had had to the house. His name was Wigglesworth, preceded by two initials she could not remember. His face, expressionless, rounded the corner and vanished. Surely she was mistaken; there are millions of men and only a few types, only a few men who aren't types. But in fear of being recognized she lowered her gaze, so as Harry had predicted, it was he who found her, though this was not Hell.

'Sally!' He was on the sunless side of I Street, hatless, his arm lifted as if for a taxi. In a business suit, he looked disconcertingly like everyone else, and as he waited at the intersection for the electric permission to walk, her stomach dipped as if she had been snapped awake two hundred miles from home. She asked herself, Who is this man? The sign said WALK. At the head of the pack, he trotted towards her; her heart thrashed. She hung helpless on the kerb while the distance between them diminished and her body, her whole hollowed body, remembered his twitchily posing hands, his hook nose that never took a tan but burned all summer long, his sad eyes of no certain colour, his crooked jubilant teeth. He grinned proudly but nervously, stood uncertain a moment, then touched her elbow and kissed her cheek. 'God, you looked great,' he said, 'swinging along, a big blonde babe without a care in the world.'

Her heart relaxed. No one else saw her this way. Not since before her father died, on a trip to San Francisco, had she felt, what she supposed all children are supposed to feel, that it was somehow wonderful of her to be, in every detail, herself.

'How on earth did you get away?'

'I just said good-bye and got in the Saab and drove to the airport.'

'You know, it's marvellous to meet a woman who can really *use* the twentieth century.' This was another fancy of his, that there was something comic and inappropriate in their living now, in this century. He took pleasure, she felt, in delicately emphasizing, in never letting her forget, the incongruities that bounded their love. His tenderness itself underlined that their love was illicit. He indulged her as one indulges a doomed child.

'Hey,' he said, calling to her across the silence. 'I don't want you to take risks for me. I want to take them for you.'

But you won't, she thought, looping her arm through his arm and bowing her head in concentration on his walking rhythm. 'Don't worry about it,' she said. 'I'm here.'

He said nothing.

'You're mad at me. I shouldn't have come.'

'I'm never mad with you. But how did you manage?'

'I managed.'

His body was mainly big bones and nerves; she felt she was holding on to a corner of a framework of a kite that was struggling to get high into the wind.

He tugged her along. He asked, 'Is Richard going to be away tonight?'

'No.'

He halted.

'Jesus, Sally. What happened? Did you just break out? Can you get back?'

His voice rose sharply, asking this last question. She blinked. Her voice came out small and scratched. 'Don't worry about it, darling. I'm here with you, and everything else seems very far away.'

'Talk to me. Don't try to shame me. If your love is bigger than mine, don't try to shame me with it. Tell me what happened.'

She told him, reliving it all, frightening herself: the beach, her panic, the children, Josie, the aeroplane, her walk, her plan to call home in an hour saying she was in Manhattan and that the Saab had broken down, refusing to start, and the Fitches had invited her to stay the night, since the art-appreciation course she was taking at the Metropolitan met tomorrow morning.

'Sweetie, it won't swing,' he told her. 'Let's try to be sane. If I put you on a plane now, you can still get back by eight.'

'Is that what you want?'

'No. You know I want you with me always.'

And, for all the evidence to the contrary, she felt this as true. She was his wife. This strange fact, unknown to the world but known to them, made whatever looked wrong right, whatever seemed foolish wise. She, Sally, was Harry's woman, and what had been precious in the first illicit trip was that in those two days she had felt this truth growing, had felt him relax. The first night, he had not slept. Several times she had been twitched awake by his gaunt body sliding from the bed, getting a drink of water, adjusting the air-conditioner, rummaging in his suitcase.

'What are you looking for?'

'My pyjamas.'

'Are you cold?'

'A little. Go to sleep.'

'I can't. You're unhappy.'

'I'm very happy. I love you.'

'But I don't keep you warm.'

'You *are* a little cooler than Ruth, somehow.'

'Really?'

Her voice must have shown that this unexpected comparison had hurt her, for he tried to retract. 'No, I don't know. Forget it. Please go to sleep.'

'I'll go back tomorrow. I won't stay tomorrow night if I give you insomnia.'

'Don't be so touchy. You don't give me insomnia. The Lord gives me insomnia.'

'Because you're sleeping with me.'

'Listen. I love insomnia. It's a proof that I'm alive.'

'Please come back to bed, Harry.' She had held on to his body, trying to drag a kite down from the sky, and herself fell asleep half-way between the earth and the dawn brightening the brick airshaft beyond their blinds. The second night, though still twitchy, he slept better, and on this, the third night, two months later, when spring had relaxed into summer, his breathing slowed and became mechanical while her heart was still lightly racing. She thought herself flattered by his trust. But early in the morning, having slept on a vague sense of loss, she awoke to a sharp deserted feeling. The room was different from the first one. The walls, though it was the same hotel, were yellow instead of white, and instead of the flower prints there were two pallid Holbein portraits. It was growing light enough beyond the blinds for her to see the faces, so dim they seemed real presences – small-mouthed, fastidious. How many perverse and drunken couplings had they been compelled to witness? A street-sweeper passed swishing on the avenue below. Their first room had given on an airshaft; this one overlooked, from five stories up, a square. Somewhere below them in the capital a collection truck whined and a trash can clattered. She thought of her milkman crossing her porch to set his bottles, clinking, inside an abandoned house. Harry lay diagonally, the sheet bunched around his throat, his feet exposed. She nudged him awake and made him passionate. In the heart of intimacy, he drowsily called her 'Ruth'. It took him a second to realize his mistake. 'Oh. I'm sorry. I don't seem to know who you are.'

'I'm Miss Sally Mathias, a crazy woman.'

'Of course you are. And you're very beautiful.'

'But a little cool, comparatively.'

'You've never forgotten that, have you?'

'No.' It fascinated her; at home, stepping into a bath, she would quickly lay fingers on her skin as if to surprise there the tepidity he had mentioned, and once, shaking Ruth's hand good-bye after a dinner party, she had held on curiously, trying to grasp the subtle caloric advantage this cool-looking woman had over her. She had noticed how Harry's skinny body often seemed feverish. Now she watched his face, and involuntarily cried out, pierced by the discovery, 'Harry, your eyes are so *sad*!'

The crooked teeth of his grin seemed Satanic. 'How can they be sad when I'm so happy?'

'They're *so* sad, Harry.'

'You shouldn't watch people's eyes when they make love.'

'I always do.'

'Then I'll close mine.'

Oh Sally, my lost only Sally, let me say now, now before we both forget, while the spark still lives on the waterfall, that I loved you, that the sight of you shamed my eyes. You were a territory where I went on tip-toe to steal a magic mirror, a hyperbolic image of my worth. I would go to meet you as a knight, to rescue you, and would become instead the dragon, and ravish you. You weighed me out in jewels, though ashes were what I could afford. Do you remember how, in our first room, on the second night, I gave you a bath and scrubbed your face and hands and long arms with the same methodical motions I used on my children? I was trying to tell you then. I was a father. Our love of children implies our loss of them. Your lids were lowered; your cheek rested on the steaming sheet of bathwater. Can I forget, forget though I live forever in Heaven among the chariots whose wheels are all eyes giving God glory, how I saw you step from a tub, your body abruptly a waterfall, a white towel tucked about your hips, your young breasts bare? Then I in turn went into the water, which your flesh had charmed into a silvery opacity, and became your child. With a drenched blinding cloth that searched out even the hollows of my ears, you, my mother, my slave, dissolved me in tender abrasions. I forgot, sank. And we dried each other's beaded backs, and went to the bed as if to sleep instantly, two obedient children dreaming in a low tent drumming with the excluded rain.

Harry closed his eyes, and it hurt her, and for the rest of the day that unfolded Sally was laid open to a vivid and frightening sense of her existence in other people's eyes. The puffylidded news vendor in the perfumed hotel lobby saw her as a spoiled young matron. The waitress who served them breakfast looked twice at the something unsettled and gingerly in the way she and Harry sat side by side, and took her for his secretary. When she relinquished Harry to a taxi and became solitary, she felt herself reflected in every glance and glass entryway. To the Japanese souvenir-store attendants she was tall. To the Negro doormen she was white. As the sun neared noon, her shadow pinched in; her hot feet hurt. Idly Sally wandered north from the hotel, through stagnant blocks of airline offices, past verdant circles where pistachio-coloured military men on horses were waving to catch her attention. Harry was to meet her at the National Gallery at one. The time until then moved forward or backward, depending on the clock she glimpsed; in the haste of her departure she had forgotten her watch. There was a gap in the tan of her arm where the watchband had been.

The iron braziers and stone vases and Asiatic paper knives in the windows of antique shops glinted back at her stupidly as she sought to find herself in them. Once she had cared about these things; once, being in a city alone had fulfilled her and coveting objects and fabrics had been a way of possessing them. Now she sought herself in bronze and silk and porcelain and was not there. When she walked with him, there was something there, but it was no longer her, it was them: her explaining to him, him to her, interchanging their lives, absorbing fractions of the immense lesson that had accumulated in the years before they had loved. She saw each thing only as something to tell him about, and without him there to listen there was nothing to tell; he had robbed her of the world. Abruptly, she became angry with him. How dare he tell her not to come and then make love to her when she did come! And then with such sad eyes beg her to feel guilty! How dare he take her free when she could sell herself for thousands to any honest man on this avenue – to that one. A foreign official with snowy cuffs and an extravagantly controlled haircut, grey-horned, preened on the burning sidewalk beside the Department of Justice Building. He was eyeing her. She was beautiful. This knowledge had been drawing near to her all morning and now it was hers. She was beautiful. Where she walked, people glanced. She was tall and blonde and big inside with love given and taken, and when, at last, she mounted the steps of the museum the gigantic scale of the rotunda did not seem inhuman but right: our inner spaces warrant palaces. She studied Charles V, as sculpted by Leone Leoni, and existed as a queen in his hyperthyroid gaze.

'Stop,' Harry said, taking her elbow from behind. 'Stop looking so beautiful and proud. You'll kill me. I'll drop dead at your feet, and how will you get the body back to Ruth?'

Ruth, Ruth: she was never out of his mind. 'I was feeling very indignant about you.'

'I know. It showed.'

'You think you know everything about me, don't you? You think you own me.'

'Not at all. You're very much your own woman.'

'No, Harry. I'm your woman. I'm sorry. I'm a burden to you.'

'Don't be sorry,' he said. 'It's a burden I need.' His eyes were watching her face for a warning, a change. 'Shall we look,' he asked timidly, 'or eat?'

'Let's look.'

Harry's enthusiasm tugged her from room to room. He had

gone to art school, and was one of those men to whom education had been an idyll, and whose occupation bore little relation to his passions. 'Here, look,' he called in a hushed cry, as if a still-life were a bird that might be startled off, 'the light; and then this, from behind the pitcher, this blue taking the blue off the cloth.' His hands demonstrated, slid hungrily through the motions of the tranquil masterpiece. People obedient to lecturing boxes plugged into their ears glared, disturbed. She must seem his student. He had found what he wanted – the wall bearing five Vermeers. 'Oh God,' he moaned, 'the drawing; people never realize how much *drawing* there is in a Vermeer. The wetness of this woman's lips. And this one, the light on her hands and the gold and the pearls. That *touch,* you know; it's a double touch – the exact colour, in the exact place.' He looked at her and smiled. 'Now you and me,' he said, 'are the exact colour, but we seem to be in the wrong place.'

'Let's not talk about us,' Sally said. 'I'm too tired to be depressed. My feet hurt, I must have walked miles this morning. Couldn't we eat?'

The cafeteria walls were hung with beady-eyed Audubon prints. Sally's stomach sank under the weight of unwelcome food. She had no appetite, which was unlike her; perhaps it was sleeplessness, perhaps the pinch of dwindling time. Whereas Harry ate briskly, to keep from talking, or in relish that another adulterous escapade was all but safely completed. They were silent together. The immense lesson she thought they had for each other felt to be fully learned.

She sighed. 'I don't know. I guess we're just terribly selfish and greedy.'

Though she had said it to please him, he disagreed. 'Do you think? After all, Richard and Ruth weren't giving us much. Why should we die just to keep their lives smooth? Quench not the spirit,' didn't St Paul say?'

'Maybe it's just the newness that makes it seem so wonderful. We'd get tired. I'm tired now.'

'Of me?'

'No. Of it.'

'I know, I know. Don't be frightened. We'll get you back safely.'

'I'm not worried about that. Richard doesn't really care.'

'He must.'

'No.'

'I don't think Ruth really cares either, if she just knew it.'

And though she knew Harry said this just to soothe her, she heard herself pressing him with, 'Do you want to not go back? Shall we just run off?'

'You'd lose your children.'

'I'm willing.'

'You say that now, but a week with me and you'd miss them and hate me because they weren't there.'

'You're so wise, Harry.'

'But it doesn't help, does it? My poor lady. You need a good man for a husband and a bad man for a lover, and you have just the opposite.'

'Richard's not such a bad man.'

'O.K. Pardon me. He's a prince.'

'I love it when you get mad at me.'

'I know you do. But I don't. I won't. I love you. If you want to fight, go home.'

She looked around at the tables – the art students, the professors with taped spectacles, the plump women escaping the heat, the birds on the walls. 'That's where I'm going,' she said.

'Yes. It's time. We'll have to stop somewhere and buy my damn kids something.'

'You *spoil* them, Harry. You'll have hardly been gone a day.'

'They expect it.' He stood up and they left, by the ground level exit. His anxious long stride hurried her past the popsicle vendors and the tourist buses, and she had no breath for words. Pitying, he took her hand, but the contact was damp and made them self-conscious; they were too old to hold hands. At the door of the drugstore displaying the usual cheap souvenirs, piggy-bank monuments and sickly Kennedyana, she panicked and refused to go in.

'Why not?' he asked. 'Help me choose.'

'No. I can't.'

'Sally.'

'Do it by yourself. They're your children – yours and Ruth's.'

His face went pale; he had never seen her like this.

She tried to make it better. 'I'll walk to the hotel and pack your suitcase. Don't worry. Please don't make me buy the toys with you.'

'Listen. I love – ' He tried to take her arm.

'Don't embarrass me, Harry. People are trying to get by.'

In walking down Fourteenth Street alone, the pavement pricking her eyes with mica, she began to cry, and realized it didn't matter, for no one was looking at her, no one at all in these multitudes.

Together they left the hotel and caught a taxi. They crossed the Potomac and passed an inexplicable wreck on the Washington Memorial Parkway. An old red Dodge with red Ohio plates had turned turtle in the middle lane, it was impossible to guess why. No other automobile seemed involved. Dozens of laughing police were redirecting traffic in the sunshine. Two fat women with dishevelled hair were embracing each other on the median strip, and the road surface glittered with glass powder. Harry's hand tightened over hers; he turned her face towards him. Then the wreck was behind them, the traffic expanded and speeded, the taxi-driver ceased muttering, and they wound their way through a maze of loops to the north terminal.

The waiting room was strangely full for the middle of a Tuesday afternoon. In all the eyes that simultaneously turned towards them Sally felt them register as a handsome couple, vaguely ordinary and vaguely striking, he in grey and she in black, he with a suitcase, she with a paperback Camus. She pictured them entering a lifetime of airports, depots, piers, and hotel lobbies, and knew that they would always look like this, tallish, young, bumping together a bit too much. She wished Harry would stop touching her; it damaged the illusion that they were married. The maintenance of this illusion did not seem to concern him. He put down his bag and walked to a waiting line, leaving her, flustered, blushing, to take a place in the adjacent line. The line was long and sluggish; it slowly dawned on Sally that the air of jocular agitation in the room did not centre around her embarrassment. She was startled – as a sleeper is startled to find upon awaking in a room whose furniture has steadfastly kept its shape throughout his long immersion in dreams – to realize that other people and other problems existed. A plump, flushed man in rumpled Dacron joined the line behind her and in sheer force of worry several times nudged her legs with his briefcase. 'I'm supposed to be in Bridgeport by seven,' he explained. His anxious face had forgotten the rakish attempt of its little blurred moustache. Once, Richard had affected such a moustache, and she wondered if that was why his upper lip seemed, in profile, so bald and vulnerable.

When the two lines wobbled close enough to touch, Harry touched her arm and said, 'Apparently the strike at Eastern has created a jam-up here. We should have thought to make reservations. What time must you be back?'

'I had thought between five and six. Don't look so *worried,* Harry.'

'I'm not worried for myself. She won't meet me until nine. Let me think. It's five after three now. Assuming we miss the three-fifteen, that puts you on the four-fifteen, your car's at La Guardia – '

'It may not start.'

She said it to tease him. But he was not amused. His long face tensed and lost the laughter wrinkles that gave it some look of maturity, of having endured. Richard had more than once remarked of Harry that he had never suffered. She took the remark to mean that Harry skimmed where Richard burrowed, or that Ruth was easier to live with than she. But it haunted her, and she wondered if that was why Harry had taken her into his life, to be taught about suffering. He said, 'Let's assume it does start. You'll be home a little after six, in the rush. Is that good enough?'

'Whatever is possible will be fine,' she said curtly. Their conversation was beginning to distract the man behind her from his own worries.

Harry tugged the money from her hand and irritably motioned her out of the line. 'I might as well buy both the damn tickets. I don't know what the hell we're trying to establish.' He looked the Bridgeport-bound man full in the face and recited, 'Travel by air, and swear'. This was like him, this impudence; he was innocently pleased to have people guess he was with a mistress.

All the waiting chairs, in the central pool of moulded plastic seats used by passengers of Delta and Piedmont and Northeast as well as United, were occupied. A young Chinese sailor rose to offer her his seat, and she stepped across his duffelbag to take it. Usually she disliked being treated as weak, but now she was willing. She wished herself away. She concentrated into the Camus. The gun in his hand, the blinding light. The Arab in dungarees. The whiplike gunshot. The unreality. Harry came to her with two yellow tickets and said, 'What a mess. Apparently there aren't any reservations to be had on anything to New York tonight; we're all standbys. But they're expecting word on an extra section any minute now. I'm sure you'll get home by six.'

'Shh. You're talking too loud.'

'Too loud for what?'

'Oh, never mind.'

Chastened, he said, 'I got these numbered boarding passes.'

'What name did you put on them?'

'Mine. O.K.?'

She had to smile. 'It seems illegal,' she said, because this was so clearly what he felt.

The loudspeaker left off a Muzak version of 'Easter Parade' and burbled unintelligibly. A fresh wave of weary travellers came down the ramp and washed up to the ticket counters. The personnel behind the counters, uniformed in aeronautic blue, seemed very young, and frightened. They stapled tickets with an exaggerated precision and answered questions in an emphatic way that reminded Sally of her own lies to Richard. 'You lie like a man,' he had once told her. 'You pick an incredible story and keep repeating it.' It touched her to remember something Richard knew about her that Harry didn't. She never lied to Harry. This realization made him seem hopelessly innocent, helpless; she went to the counter herself, bypassing the lines of agitated men. There must be some advantage to being a woman; it can't be all waiting and wanting. There was a girl with hair bleached white handling the tickets. The girl was so young she dared whiten her hair, and abruptly Sally felt haughty towards her, a woman above her. This child had no children, no married lover she could not marry. 'I *must* get home by six o'clock,' Sally told her. But her voice came out fragile and shy, whereas the girl's in answering was professionally firm.

'I'm sorry, Miss,' she said. 'The next La Guardia plane departs at four-fifteen. Standbys are advised to be at Gate 27 with their numbered boarding passes.'

'But will we get on?' Sally asked.

'The next scheduled flight to La Guardia is at four-fifteen,' the girl repeated, stapling a ticket smartly.

Harry had come up behind Sally. 'We were told there would be a section.'

'We're waiting for word on that, sir,' the girl said. Her doll-like eyes, cleverly enlarged by the company's official make-up, took in Harry and Sally together but did not change expression. Sally wondered if she should say 'we' or 'I'. Other people, overhearing the conversation and scenting preferred treatment, had begun to bunch behind them. 'Hold your lines, please,' the girl called, her voice rising. 'Please do not get out of line.' She was frightened. Suddenly Sally felt only sympathy for this girl. While she and Harry had been making love, children had been compelled to assume management of the world. And now the grown-ups, returning from their selfish beds, were angry to find that the world had fallen apart: how greedy we all are, how pushing! Ashamed, Sally closed her eyes and wished she were herself a child. A child before her father failed to return from that trip. All trips, she saw, have that possibility, of no return.

'I'm thirsty,' she said.

Harry asked, 'What sort of thirsty? For a real drink or just for anything?'

'Just anything. A drink might make me dizzier still.' A part of her was still back on the beach with Meursault.

The hot-dog counter was too crowded to besiege, but a hundred steps down the corridor towards the main terminal they found a bar, wide open on one side like a stage, with an empty table in a far corner. Harry coaxed two wax-paper cubes of milk from a reluctant Cuban ensconced behind two bubbling urns of coloured water. Coming to her at the table, Harry set one carton on his head and balanced it, and waved a white-wrapped drinking straw at her like a magic wand. She was Cinderella.

She said, 'Don't be an exhibitionist.'

'I am,' he said. 'I'm a terrible person, I've decided. I can't imagine what you see in me.'

She pried up the dotted corner and inserted the straw and sipped; she knew by the edge in his face that he was going to talk.

'Let's analyse this,' he said. 'What do you see in me? It must be that you can have me only for moments, moments you have to fight for, and this makes them seem precious. Now, if we got married, if I crushed my wife and waded through my children's blood for you – '

'That's a horrible thing to say, Harry.'

'It's the way I see it. If I did this, I'd no longer be the man you think you love. I'd be the kind of man who abandons his wife and three children. I'd despise myself, and quite quickly you'd concur.'

'I'm not so sure that's how it works,' she said, trying to fit her impressions of life into some sort of generalization. Harry really didn't know. He believed in choices, in mistakes, in damnation, in the avoidance of suffering. She and Richard believed simply that things happened. After everything was said about how unhappy her childhood had been – her father's death, her mother's coldness, the succession of boarding schools – there remained her sense that she would, now, be less of a person if it had happened any other way. She would be somebody else, somebody she had no desire to be.

'On the other hand,' he said, cocking his wrist elegantly – he took more pleasure in his hands than anyone she had ever known – 'why do I love you? Well, you're gorgeous, brave, kind – really so kind – alive, female, and all the rest of it that anybody can see. To this extent, anyone who sees you come into a room loves you. The first time I saw you, I loved you, and you were eight months pregnant with Peter.'

'You're wrong, though. Very few people like me.'

He reflected a moment, as if reviewing the hearts of their common acquaintances, and then said, with his abrasive dispassion, 'You may be right.'

'You're really the only man who sees me as very special.' Her chin trembled; saying it, she felt it clinched her claim on him.

He said, 'Other men are stupid. Anyway, in addition to your evident charms, you are unhappy. You need me and I can't give myself to you. I want you and I can't have you. You're like a set of golden stairs I can never finish climbing. I look down, and the earth is a little blue mist. I look up, and there's this radiance I can never reach. It gives you your incredible beauty, and if I marry you I'll destroy it.'

'You know, Harry, a marriage makes something, too. It isn't all destroying illusions.'

'I know that. I do know that. It kills me. I want, part of all this is, I want to *shape* you, to make you all over again. I feel I could. I don't feel this with Ruth. Somehow, she's formed, and the best kind of life I can live with her will be lived in' –

his fingers illustrated the word in the air – 'parallel.'

'Let's face it, Harry. You still love her quite a bit.'

'I don't dislike her, it's a fact. I wish I did. It might make it easier.'

Her straw sucked air from the bottom of the carton. 'Shouldn't we be going out to catch this four-fifteen?'

'Don't shut me up quite yet. Please. Listen. I see it so clearly. What we have, sweet Sally, is an ideal love. It's ideal because it can't be realized. As far as the world goes, we don't exist. We've never kissed, we've never made love, we haven't been in Washington together; we're ghosts. And any attempt to stop being ghosts, to move out of this pain, will kill us. Oh, we could make a mess and get married and patch up a life together – it's done in the papers every day – but what we have now, we'd lose. Of course, the sad thing is we're going to lose it anyway. This is just too much of a strain for you. You're going to start hating me.' He seemed pleased at this perfect conclusion.

'Or you me,' she said, rising. She didn't like this place. Some children squabbling at another table made her miss her own. Their mother, though younger than she, looked exhausted forever.

As they left the stage-shaped bar, Harry laughed to himself so theatrically that heads turned around. He seized her arm and said, 'You know what we're like? It just came to me. We're like the Lord's Prayer written on the edge of a knife. Remember, as a kid, how in Ripley's "Believe It or Not!" there were always things like that? Done by an old Cherokee engraver in Stillwater, Oklahoma?'

They walked down the poster-lined corridor, painted blue along one wall and cream along the other, to the departure gates. Sally felt weak under his torrent – disarmed, somehow, and ridiculed. 'Harry, our marriage would be like other marriages, it wouldn't be wonderful every minute, but that doesn't mean it wouldn't be good.'

'Oh, don't,' he moaned, his eyes colourless. 'Don't make me grieve. Of course it would be good. My God. Of course you'd be a better wife for me than Ruth. Just on your animal merits alone.'

Animal – the word stung, but why? It was exact. At Gate 27 the animals had packed themselves like cattle in a chute, and they smelled of panic. For the first time, Sally felt the blindness of the situation. Dozens had arrived ahead of them. The illusion of order maintained by the curt young ticket-sellers in the ample waiting room disintegrated out here among the strident posters for Bermuda, for the *Washington Post,* and New York musicals with fey titles. No airline employee was in sight. The steel door of Gate 27 was shut tight, like a gas chamber. The concrete floor tipped, as if to drain blood. Harry set down his suitcase near the corrugated wall and motioned her to sit on it, then left her to go and talk to the men at the head of the crush. He came back to say, 'Gee, two of those guys have been waiting since noon.'

'Do you have those numbered passes?' she asked.

He rummaged, distraught and limp, through all his pockets twice before finding them; then snapped them into view like a magician. An invisible loudspeaker barked. A Negro in big blue sunglasses and a pilot's cap opened the steel door from the other side. A little narrow-faced purser huddled close to him. The loudspeaker announced the boarding at Gate 27 of the four-fifteen flight to La Guardia, and a serene parade, with lightweight suitcases, well-dressed children, and flowered hats, came down the corridor. These were the people with reservations. The rest of them, the standbys, were herded to the other side of the pipe railing. One by one, the reservations were checked through at the desk and disappeared. A crescendo of complaint from the jam of standbys threatened the Negro in blue sunglasses; he looked up from tearing tickets and flashed an exhilarating grin, a great smile dazzling in the depth of its pleasure, its vengeance, its comprehension, its angelic scorn. 'Keep cool, men,' he said. 'Let the wife get him out of the house.'

Disproportionate laughter answered this jest. Harry laughed

too, and looked down at her warily, and she was disgusted; they were toadying to the Negro with their laughter. That he had noticed them at all gave them hope of passing through the gate. The gate had become something shameful that they must bribe and beg to enter. When the last of the reservations were checked through, there was a consultation at the desk and two numbers were read off, numbers which had no relation to the numbers Harry and Sally held. Two men, the mysterious elect, in costume and appearance no different from the others, detached themselves from the pack and passed through. The Negro lifted his blue sunglasses and slowly gazed at the remaining faces. His eyes were dark, gentle, and bloodshot. They rested a moment on Sally, who had risen from sitting. 'That's it, friends,' he said.

A guttural moan of protest went up. 'What about a section?' a man shouted. The Negro didn't seem to hear. He sidestepped, and the steel door clanged shut behind him. A phalanx of people who had embarked farther down the corridor marched into them, and were all forced back into the waiting room, which had grown smaller. Sally's heels ached, her throat felt dry again, and the man beside her appeared painted and strange, both close and far, like, in a school play, another girl playing the part of her husband. His gathering fright, which she could scent, insulted her. She told him, 'Harry, you're not seeing the humour of it.'

He asked, 'Shall we try American?'

'I don't have enough money for another ticket.'

'Jesus, neither do I. I'll have to trade ours in.'

He stood in the long line for fifteen minutes, and, their money returned, they raced down the long rats'-passage of corridors and stairways that connected the north and main terminals. The American Airlines quarters were on the far side. They were larger and more subtly lit, but the slick surfaces had not repelled the plague of confusion. Coming away from the ticket desks were several familiar faces, other veterans of the wait. 'No soap, kids,' one man called to them cheerfully. So they were known. They must be conspicuous; did they look so illicit? Did they stink so of love?

The American ticket agent, speaking like a recording, confirmed the bad news; no space north until tomorrow morning. Harry turned, his mouth puckered distastefully under his peeling nose.

Sally asked, 'Can we get our United tickets back? We still have our passes.'

'I doubt it. Oh, I am incompetent. You better get a pilot for a lover.'

They raced back, her blistered heels crying out at every step, and Harry stood in line again, and the girl with artificially white hair, sighing, sold him back their tickets. He returned to Sally and told her, 'She says there's no point in trying to board the five-fifteen, but they expect a section to be ready by six. Will Richard be home?'

'I suppose. Harry, don't look so wild. It can't be helped. Let's just accept these extra hours together.'

His hands hung exhausted at his sides. He reached for her arm. 'Let's go for a walk.'

They walked past machines vending candy bars and Harold Robbins, and pushed through a besmirched double door into the open air. She took off her shoes and he carried them one in each hand. She took his arm and he shifted a shoe to his coat pocket so one of his hands could hold one of hers. They found a long pavement, down in front of some faceless low brick buildings, where apparently no one ever walked, and walked a distance down this pavement. The cement was warm to her stockinged feet. Harry sighed and sat on a cement step between two patches of weary grass that needed mowing. She sat down beside him. They looked across a no man's land of raw earth where a solitary bulldozer rested tilting, as if abandoned in the middle of a lurch on the stroke ending the working day. An air of peace hung above these scraped acres. Beyond, a filament of highway bridge silently glittered with the passage of cars. There were trees, and some reddish rows of government housing, and a distant plantation manse on a low blue ridge, and an immense soft sky going green above the hushed horizon. It was a landscape of unexpected benevolence. Her toes felt cool out of her shoes, and her man regained his reality in the presence of air and grass.

'I see us,' he said stretching his arm towards the distance, 'in Wyoming, with your children, and a horse, and a cold little lake we can swim in, and a garden we can make near the house.'

She laughed. She had once said, in passing, that she had always wanted to return to the West, but not to the Coast, and he had built their whole future on it. 'Wyoming', where neither of them had ever been, was them together, was happiness, outdoors, marriage. 'Wyoming' – the very word, when she wrote it to herself, seemed open and free. 'Don't tease me,' she said.

'Do I tease you? I don't mean to. I say these things because I feel them, I want them. I'm sorry. I'm afraid I'm not very strong with you; I guess I should pretend I don't think it would be wonderful. But it would be wonderful, if I could swallow the guilt. We'd spend the first month making love and looking at things. We'll be very tired when we get there, and we'll have to start looking at the world all over again, and rebuild it from the bottom up, beginning with the pebbles.'

She laughed. 'Is that what we'd do?'

He seemed hurt. 'No? Doesn't that make sense? I always want land after making love to you. This morning, stepping into the street with you, I saw a little plant in the window of a restaurant, and it was terribly vivid to me. Every leaf, every vein. It's the way I saw things in art school.'

'Tell me about art school, Harry.'

'There's nothing to tell. I went there, and met Ruth, and she painted quite well in a feminine way, and her father was a minister, and I married her. I'm not sorry. We had good years.'

'You know, you'd miss her.'

'In ways, perhaps. You'd miss Richard, oddly enough.'

'Don't say "oddly enough", Harry. Sometimes you make me feel its all my doing. You and Ruth were happy – '

'No.'

' – and along came this miserable woman pretending she wanted a lover when what she really wanted was you for a husband.'

'No. Listen. I loved you for years. You know that. It didn't take our sleeping together to tell me that I loved you; it was the way you *looked*. As to marriage, you weren't the one who brought it up. You assumed it was impossible. It was I who thought it might be possible. It was weak of me to mention it before I was sure, but even that, I did out of love for you; I wanted you to know – Oh, I talk too much. The word "love" is beginning to sound nonsensical.'

'You've done one thing wrong, Harry.'

'What's that? I've done everything wrong.'

'In making me feel so loved you've convinced me being somebody's mistress is too shabby for me.'

'It is. You're too nice, you're too straight, really. You give too completely. I hate myself for accepting.'

'Accept, Harry. If you can't take me as a wife, don't spoil me as a mistress.'

'But I don't *want* you as a mistress; our lives just aren't built for it. Mistresses exist in European novels. Here, there's no institution except marriage. Marriage and the Friday-night basketball game. You can't take this indefinitely; you think you can, but I know you can't. I know you.'

'I guess I know it too. It's just that I'm so scared of trying for everything and losing what we have.'

'But what we have must become fruitful, or it will grow bored and go away. I don't mean having babies, I mean just being relaxed, and, you know, with a blessing. Does "blessing" seem silly to you?'

'Can't we give each other the blessing?'

'No. For some reason it must come from above.'

Above them, in a sky still bright though shadows like grain for harvest were gathering on the earth, an aeroplane hung cruciform, silver, soundless. He put his arm lightly around her shoulders and looked at her in a different mood; his face broke into its fatherly smile, forgiving, enveloping. He said, 'Hey', and looked at his knees. 'You know, I can sit here with you and talk about loss, about my losing you, and us losing our love, but I can do it only because you're with me, so it doesn't seem serious. When I have lost you, when you're not there, it's a fantastic ache. Just fantastic. And everything that keeps me from coming to you seems just words.'

'But it's not just words.'

'No. Not quite, I guess. Maybe our trouble is that we live in the twilight of the old morality, and there's just enough to torment us, and not enough to hold us in.'

The timbre of his voice, dipping towards some final shadow, chilled her. She moved forward out from under his arm, stood up, inhaled, and let her mind expand into the landscape. 'What a beautiful long day,' she said, trying to recapture their pleasure in discovering this place.

'Almost the longest of the year,' he said, rising with the pert little dignity he put on when he felt rebuffed. 'I can't remember if the days are drawing in now, or still opening up.' He looked at her, imagined she didn't understand, and explained, 'The solstice.' Both laughed, because he had explained the obvious.

They returned to the waiting room and found it still full. The five-fifteen had departed. The aroma of hot dogs had thickened; it was supper time. The three young people behind the counters had grown bored with the indefatigable emergency. They passed wisecracks back and forth between them, shrugged a great deal, and did not so much answer as indulge the angry press of anxiety before them. The girl with white hair was sipping coffee from a paper cup. Harry asked her if the six-o'clock section was ready yet.

'We have not yet received word, sir.'

'But you said an hour ago there would be one.'

'It will be announced, sir, as soon as definite word is received.'

'But we *have* to get home. Our – our baby-sitter has to go to a dance.' How like Harry, Sally thought, to lie, when he did lie, so badly. A dance on a Tuesday night? She and the girl looked at each other, and Harry, exposed between them, nakedly asked the girl, 'Is there any hope?'

'We have requested a section from the head office and are awaiting word,' the girl said, and turned her back to sip her coffee in privacy.

Harry looked so grim that Sally told him, 'I'm hungry', hoping to elicit one of his rude friendly jokes about her appetite. But he accepted the statement simply, as a responsibility, and, heavily retrieving his suitcase from behind a plastic chair, led her back through the blue and cream corridor to the bar. All the tables were full. He put the suitcase by a metal post and had her sit on it while he went to ask if they had sandwiches. He returned with two in wax paper and two paper cups of coffee. Why not a real drink? Perhaps he thought it would be indecent, or that they needed to keep their wits. Richard right now would be bringing her a gin and tonic, or a Martini, or a Daiquiri, or even a rum Collins or a gin daisy. She had bought him a cocktail shaker for their first Christmas, and in even their bitterest times he would ceremoniously bring her a sweet drink.

Harry ate standing above her, and the pose revived the actor in him. If the area was a stage, they were on the very lip. A constant shuffle of people passed a few feet from them. 'I've figured out the bind I'm in,' he told her. 'It's between death and death. To live without you is death to me. On the other hand, to abandon my family is a sin; to do it I'd have to deny God, and by denying God I'd give up all claim on immortality.'

Sally felt weak; what could she say to such an accusation? She tried to fit herself into his frame of mind; she could hardly believe that minds still existed in that frame.

Having gobbled his sandwich, he squatted, and murmured to her. She turned her head aside in embarrassment, and caught a familiar-looking man gazing at them from over by the bar. He averted his gaze; his little moustache, profiled against a neon advertisement, made a dab of green light under his nose. Harry was murmuring, 'I look at your face, and imagine myself lying in bed dying, and ask myself, "Is this the face I want at my death-bed?" And I don't know. I honestly *don't know,* Sally.'

'You're not going to die for a long time, Harry, and you'll have many women after me.'

'I will *not.* You are my only woman, you're the only woman I want. You were given to me in Heaven, and Heaven won't let me have you.'

She felt he enjoyed making things impossible by carrying them into these absurd absolutes. Yet she knew also that he did it like a child who states the worst, hoping to be contradicted. 'You're not a woman, Harry, so I think you exaggerate what your leaving would do to Ruth.'

'Really? What would it do? Tell me.' Ruth was the one earthly topic that never failed to interest him.

'Well, she'd be stunned, and very lonely, but she'd have the children, and she'd have – this is hard to say, but I remember it from the times I've been alone – she'd have the satisfaction of getting through every day by herself. It's something marriage doesn't give you. And then, of course, she would remarry.'

'Do you think she would? Say yes.'

'Of course she would. But – Harry? Now don't get mad.'

'I'm listening.'

'You ought to do it if you're going to do it. I don't know how much she guesses, or how much you tell her, but if you torture her the way you torture me – '

'Do I torture you? God. I mean to do just the opposite.'

'I know. But it – I . . . I don't want to sell myself. I'll come to you as long as I can, and you don't have to marry me. But you mustn't keep teasing me with the possibility. If it's possible, and you want it, do it, Harry; leave her, and let her make a new life. She'll live.'

'I wish I was sure of that. If only there was some decent man who I know would marry her and take care of her – but every man we know, compared to me, is a clunk. Really. I'm not conceited, but that's a fact.'

She wondered if that was why she loved him – that he could say something like that, and still look boyish, and expectant, and willing to be taught. 'She won't find another man until you leave her,' Sally told him. 'You can't pick her new husband for her, Harry; now that *is* conceited of you.'

Whenever she tried to puncture him, he seemed grateful. *Come on,* his grin seemed to say, *hurt me. Help me.* 'Well,' he said, and put his coffee cup inside hers. 'This has been very interesting. We're just full of home truths.'

'I guess we're talked out,' she said, trying to apologize.

'It's nice, isn't it? It would be so nice, for us to have said everything, and just be quiet together. But we'd better go back. Back to Pandemonium.'

Standing up, she said, 'Thank you for the sandwich. It was very good.'

He told her, 'You're great. You're a great blonde. When you get up, it's like the flag being raised. I want to pledge allegiance.' And in front of everyone he solemnly placed his hand over his heart.

The crowd had swelled; around the ticket counters it was impenetrable. The enormous hopelessness of their position broke upon her, and for the first time since noon Sally wanted to cry. Harry turned to her and said, 'Don't worry. I'll get you home. What about renting a car?'

'And driving all that way? Harry, how *can* we?'

'Well, don't you feel we've had it, plane-wise?'

She nodded, and tears burned in her throat like a small regurgitation. Harry virtually ran; the skin of her heels seemed to be tearing loose as she chased him down the corridor. The automobile-rental booths were far away, three lonely islands side by side.

The Hertz girl wore yellow, the Avis girl red, the National girl green. Harry had a Hertz credit card, and the girl in yellow said, 'I'm sorry, all our cars have been taken. Everybody wants to go to New York.'

It was their destiny to be late. Everywhere they went, crowds had been before them. Harry protested ineffectually; indeed, he seemed relieved to have one more possibility closed, one more excuse for inaction provided. Richard would somehow have managed; nothing was too complicated for him to finagle, finagling was a sensuous pleasure for him. Richard's shape, stocky but quick, moved in the corner of her eye; a man came up to them and said, 'Did I hear you say New York? I'd be happy to share expenses with you.' He was the man who had to be in Bridgeport by seven o'clock. It was nearly seven now.

The girl at Hertz called across the aisle to the girl at Avis, 'Gina, do you have any more cars you can let go to New York?'

'I doubt it but let me call the lot.' Gina dialled, bracing the receiver between her shoulder and ear.

The tall green girl at the National desk asked, 'Why does everybody want to go to New York? What's in New York?'

'The Liberty Bell,' Harry told her.

'If I were you two,' she said to him, 'I'd take a cab back into the city and see a show.'

Harry asked her, 'What's good?'

The Hertz girl said, 'My boyfriend and I had a nice time at *Bonnie and Clyde*.'

'We've seen it,' Harry said. 'We kind of hated it. It was like a golf ball, with blue goo in the middle.' It saddened Sally to see how easily he talked to women, any women.

Gina put down the phone and said, 'Alice, they have one just came in they'll let go.'

And Alice, sweet chinless Alice with her easily pleased

boyfriend, smiled bucktoothed and said, 'There you are, sir. She'll take care of you.'

'Don't forget me,' the man who had to go to Bridgeport said.

Harry turned to the man, blushed, and explained, 'My wife and I, I guess, would prefer to drive alone.'

The man stepped forward and shook Harry's hand. 'My name's Fancher. I make my home in Elizabeth, New Jersey, and I'm in the chemical-products line. I don't want to pressure you one way or another, but it would be a great kindness to me if I could ride along.'

Harry gracefully clapped his long hand to the top of his head and said, 'Well, let's think about it. Let me get the car first.'

He dropped his Hertz credit card on Gina's desk and she, handsome but coarse-skinned, petulantly explained that since this was an Avis car she would need a cash deposit of twenty-five dollars.

'But we don't have twenty-five dollars, do we?' Harry asked Sally.

'The tickets,' she said.

Fancher stepped forward. 'You want twenty-five dollars?'

She and Harry studied each other, and the romance of driving together alone under moonlight, towards midnight and their doom, hung between them like a painted screen. 'I'll cash in the tickets,' he said. 'I'll turn that girl's hair really grey.' To Gina he said, 'I'll be back in ten minutes.' To Sally he said, 'You wait here and guard the car.' He winced apologetically in Fancher's face and flew away.

Long minutes passed. Mr Fancher stayed with her silently, touching his moustache, guarding her while she guarded the phantom automobile. The three girls, in the lull that had settled over their islands, chatted back and forth, about boyfriends and bathing suits. Sally felt dizzy. The acid taste kept rising in her throat; she felt sick of love. Love, love was what had clogged the world, it was love that refused to let the planes leave, love that hid her children from her, love that made her husband look senile in profile. Fancher hovered close to her; he was in the chemical-products line and should be in Bridgeport, yet she had promised to love and obey this man till death did them part. *Dear God, let go.* She held herself very upright and quiet, wondering if she would throw up. The cement floor was littered with cigarette filters and heel marks. The green girl from National was saying that she didn't think she had the right figure for a bikini, being so tall, but her boyfriend got her one for a joke, and now she wouldn't wear anything else, it felt so free.

Red from running, Harry came back, Harry with his sunburned nose and elusive eyes and his beautiful look of being a kite. 'Forget it,' he announced, making a triumphant V with his arms, and including all four women in his emblematic embrace. To Fancher he said, 'You can have the car. Good luck in Bridgeport.' He touched Sally's arm and told her, 'The girl at United says there's going to be a section and to see a name she gave me.' He showed her a slip of paper on which a hasty female hand had scribbled the one word 'Cardomon'.

'Have you seen him yet?'

'No, he wasn't there at the moment. Let's go back and find him.'

'Harry, your suitcase.'

'Oh. Right. God, you're so competent, Sally.'

Fancher said, 'You said there's a section? Then I don't want the car either.' He knifed past them and, moving with a quickness surprising in a stout man, beat them back to the waiting room.

Here an instinct of movement seemed to have seized the human tides; almost all the people were moving towards the boarding gates. Harry and Sally, alarmed, followed them out of the doors and down the corridor. A crowd had already accumulated. A strange chant was going up; it seemed to Sally to be 'The bridesmaid, the bridesmaid'. She thought it was another hallucination, but it proved to be exactly what they were shouting. At the core of the crowd, the Negro in blue sunglasses was conferring with a sandy-haired man wearing a company coat and carrying a clipboard. Beside them, a shinily dressed arc of the middle-aged was pressing forward, with deep Dixie accents, a girl in a flowered hat and a shimmering dress of yellow silk. Sally understood: she was a bridesmaid, and had to be on the plane or miss a wedding: or had she come from a wedding? The chant deepened. Harry joined in. 'The bridesmaid, the bridesmaid!' Indignation bit into Sally's stomach, and the press of tears overwhelmed her eyes. What was so unfair, the girl was not even pretty. She had a strawberry birthmark beside her nose and a tense wrinkled simper. The sandy man nodded to the Negro, who flashed his deep ironic smile and took the bridesmaid's ticket. A cheer went up. The girl passed through the door. The gate clanged shut. The seven-fifteen flight to New York had departed.

Back in the waiting room, Harry left Sally and went to look for Mr Cardomon. As she stood alone by the tired blue wall, a tall man came up to her and said gently, 'Aren't you Sally Mathias?'

It was Two Initials Wigglesworth. The two initials abruptly came to her: A. D. He asked, 'Are you here with Dick?' He spoke with velvet smoothness; he was very well-shaped and very combed, and so wealthy that Richard had fairly danced the few times he had come to the house.

'No, I'm here by myself,' she said. 'I do this every so often. My mother lives in Georgetown. Are you trying to get to New York?'

'No, I'm going to St Louis. My plane leaves in half an hour. Could I get you a drink?'

'That would be lovely,' Sally said, 'but I'm a standby and I think I'd better stay here. We're waiting for a section.' She adjusted the pronoun. 'I've been here since three o'clock. It's a grotesque mess.'

'I do think you could use a drink.' He smiled like a great brushed cat purring – he was perfectly handsome and perfectly repulsive, and beneath all his grooming he knew it.

'I think I could too,' she said, glancing around for Harry. He wasn't anywhere.

Wigglesworth interpreted her glancing around as acquiescence, and took her arm. She snapped it away. She hadn't realized how tense she was. 'I'm sorry,' she said. 'I'm honestly on the verge of tears; Richard expected me back by supper.'

'It makes one rather miss the dear old trains, doesn't it?' he said soothingly, offended.

'What are you going to do in St Louis?' she asked. She felt the tight mask of charm fitting across her face; felt herself unstoppably beginning to flirt.

'Oh, very dreary. Banking business, a rail merger. I loathe the Midwest.'

'Do you?'

'Tell me, how did Dick do with his Canadian oil issue? I was fascinated, but I couldn't interest Father.'

'I never heard about it. He never tells me anything. How is Bea?' She had been groping for his wife's name, remembering only the woman's waxen ballerina's face and that her name, too, was some sort of initial.

'*Very* well. We have two children now.'

'*Do* you? That's wonderful. Another girl?'

'Another boy. Are you sure you wouldn't like that drink?'

'It's tempting,' Sally said.

'Have you heard about Perry Carter? He's married again – a charming Indonesian girl. She does simultaneous translation at the U.N.'

'Yes. That would amuse him.'

Wigglesworth laughed; his teeth were immaculate, but small for his face. 'And Bink Hubbard – I know Richard has met him – has disappeared in Florida; the rumour has it he's shipped out on a Liberian freighter again.'

'I don't think I know him.'

'No, you wouldn't. He's one of those men other men rather envy.'

'Yes, there is that kind of man.' Sally sounded mechanical

to herself: a social machine that went push, pull, push, pull.

Wigglesworth gazed over her head and asked, 'Isn't that Harry Conant?'

'Where? Do you know Harry?'

'Of course. Doesn't he live rather near you?'

'We don't see them very often. How do you know him?'

He glanced down, eyebrows lifted at the intensity of her concern. 'Through Ruth,' he said. 'My parents went to her father's church. She was considered quite a beauty.'

'She still is.'

Harry, hesitating in the side of her vision, came close, and announced, 'Anno Domini Wigglesworth, the Rock of Ages himself.'

'Harry. Are you stranded here too?'

'Apparently. I've just been looking for a mythical man called Cardomon who's supposed to unstrand us.'

'You and Mrs Mathias?'

'Yes, Mrs Mathias and I seem to be caught in the same box.' He looked down at his hand, which held two tickets. He held them up. 'I've taken over negotiations for her. Do you have a reservation?'

'Yes.'

'You would. Would you like to give it to Sally?'

'I'm going the wrong way, to St Louis.'

Harry turned to Sally and said, 'Maybe we should go to St Louis. We could get on a raft and float down the Mississippi.'

She laughed, shocked. How dare he tease her, right in the teeth of disaster!

Wigglesworth's smile had become fixed, and from the heightened composure of both men's faces she knew she had become an object, a body, between them. 'I was just telling Sally,' Wigglesworth said, 'that Perry Carter has married an Indonesian.'

'Excellent,' Harry said. 'Miscegenation is the only cure for world tension. Make love, not war.'

'Come, Harry,' the other man said. 'When did you get

religion? I thought you were stooging for the State Department.'

They were fighting over her. Sally's sick dread returned, a desire to sleep; she thought of Richard sitting alone, puzzled, worried for her, sipping his second Martini, and yearned to faint, to sink down into the dirty grey floor, into the spaces between the cigarette filters, and awake at his feet. The men talked on, bantering angrily through her daze, until Wigglesworth, routed by Harry's superior rudeness, said, 'I believe it's time for me to board. Good luck to both of you.' And in his farewell, in the way he bowed from his rigid height, there was something genuinely gracious, almost a blessing. Only a stuffed shirt could have brought it off.

Harry was sulky and opaque. Had it come, his hating her? She asked him, 'You didn't find Cardomon?'

'No. He doesn't exist. Do you think it's a code? Cardomon spelled backwards is Nom-o-drac.' The St Louis flight was announced and Wigglesworth, staring straight ahead, chin high, was carried out of the waiting room on a stream of briefcases. Harry took Sally's hand. 'You're trembling.'

'A little. That upset me.'

'Does he see Richard often?'

'Almost never. He snubs Richard.'

'He won't say anything. There'd be no percentage in it for him. He'll save this on the chance he can use it with you.'

'He's right, isn't he? I mean, what he saw me as, I am.'

'What did he see you as?'

'Don't make me say it, Harry.'

Harry mulled this refusal. 'Actually,' he said, 'you'd be much better off with him than with me. He'd get you on a goddam plane, I know that.'

'Harry.'

'Mm?'

'Don't blame yourself. You told me not to come.'

'But I wanted you to come. You knew that. That's why you came.'

'I came for myself, too.'

He sighed. 'Oh, Sally,' he said. 'You're so kind to me.' He looked at the tickets in his hand and put them into his side coat pocket and looked up at her wearily. A little smile of regret brightened his face. 'Hey?'

'Hi.'

'Let's get married.'

'Please, Harry.'

'No, let's. The hell with this. We can't get back. God has spoken.'

'I don't think you mean it.'

His voice was listless. 'No. I do. You act like a wife to me. You look like Mrs Conant to me.'

'But I'm not, Harry. I'd like to be.'

'O.K., then. Proposal accepted. I don't see any other way but to go back to the hotel and call up Ruth and Richard and eventually get married. It's the only thing I can think of. I'm tired, right now, but I think I'll be very happy.'

'I'll try to make you happy.'

'I think we can get your children. The courts don't really care who commits the adultery any more.'

'Are you sure it's what you want?'

'Of course. I didn't think it would come quite this way, but I'm glad it's come.' Still he didn't move. She waited there beside him, her heart a perfect blank. Joy and sorrow, fear and hope – all the things that had been crowding upon her had dispersed. There was even an empty space of floor around them. People were clamouring and gesturing, but she heard only silence. She became aware that she was thirsty and that the blisters on her heels hurt. She could take off her shoes in the hotel room. Later, they could get a drink in the bar.

The girl with unnaturally white hair advanced into the empty space around them. 'Mr and Mrs Conant? I've found Mr Cardomon.' She was followed by a sandy man wearing an airlines jacket and carrying a clipboard. Sally had seen him before; when?

Harry lurched explosively away from her. He pulled out his tickets. They were tattered and looked worthless. He explained, stammering, 'We've been trying to get on a New York plane since three this afternoon and turned down a car rental because we were told there was going to be a section.'

Mr Cardomon asked, 'Could I have your numbered standby passes?' While he examined them, he rubbed the underside of his nose with a knuckle. Then he examined both their faces, constantly returning his fingers to the itch on his nose. Sally felt that she and the white-haired girl were standing on tiptoe. A tender, very distant scent of sweat came to her from Harry's neck. Mr Cardomon wrote on the clipboard, saying to himself, 'Conant, two'. Then he lifted up his youthful head of sandy curly hair and showed Sally that his eyes were grey, the colour of aluminium. He knew everything. He told Harry, 'Miss March will staple boarding passes to your tickets.'

'You mean there *is* a plane?' Harry asked.

Cardomon looked at his wristwatch. 'It should be leaving in thirty minutes, from Gate 28.'

'And we're *on* it? My God, thank you. *Thank* you. We had just decided to go back to the hotel.' And, unable to convey his gratitude sufficiently to Mr Cardomon, who had turned his back, Harry turned to the girl and gushed, 'You know, I've grown to love your hair. Don't ever dye it back.'

He went off with her and came back with two blue squares stapled to the tickets and picked up his suitcase containing toys for his children and walked with Sally down the corridor. She knew all the posters by now. Shows she would not see, islands she would not visit. An apprehensive mob, scenting redemption, had gathered at Gate 28, and in time the Negro appeared, his sunglasses tucked into his shirt pocket, and slowly, enjoying it, read off a list of names. Theirs was the last name on the list. Conant. They passed through the gate, and in glancing behind her Sally thought she saw, amid the press of those who had been left behind, the worried jaunty face that should have been in Bridgeport.

The plane was a little DC-3 with a steep tilt to its aisle. Inside, all the men, coats off, briefcases tucked away, were laughing. 'I wonder what attic they got this out of,' one man called, and Harry laughed, and tapped her bottom. His delight and relief were so vivid she tried to share them, but she had little capacity for sharing left. She took the inside seat and through the oval window studied the mechanics waving flashlights while Harry stroked her arms and begged to be praised for having got them a plane. She thought of the Camus in her pocketbook and closed her eyes. Her painful shoes slipped off. Behind her she could hear a stewardess talking, and below her window a machine whined. It was chilly in the plane, as if it had been brought to them from a great cold height. Harry laid something over her – his suit coat. The collar rubbed her chin. He stroked her arms and the backs of her hands and she felt the metal curving close around her; men were murmuring and she was the only woman in the plane and Harry's coat smelled faintly of him and she was nearly asleep before the plane moved.

Oh, Sally, it was such a beautiful ride! Do you remember at what a low altitude we flew? How our little plane, like a swan boat mildly bobbing in an occasional current, carried us through the middle air that was spangled with constellations above and cities below? I saw, past the halo of your sleeping hair, the capital's continent of light expand, tilt, and expand again: Dante could not have dreamed such a rose. Our DC-3, fetched from Heaven knows where to carry us home, was chilly – unheated, unpressurized; it was honest ether we inhaled. We floated, our two engines beating liquidly, just high enough to be high, across Baltimore, the Chesapeake Bay, New Jersey dark with farms. Any higher, and we could not have seen each forked car sliding home, each house embedded in its frame of light. Each bridge was a double strand of diamonds, each road-house a sunken ruby, each town a scarf of pearls. And the stars level with our windows rode along motionless to keep us company. Never have I endured such beauty.

And it was you, your beauty. Through you I had entered this firmament. You seemed, asleep beside me while the band of men guarding us rustled newspapers and accepted coffee, you seemed – what? You were not my wife, you were not my sister, nor my child. I stroked your forearms to tell you, even in your sleep, that I was there. Your arms seemed wonderfully long, Sally; your physical size as you slept was a great pride to me. How proud I was, for the hour and more that it took our pilot to pedal our quaint craft from metropolis to metropolis, to be your guard. Never before, never since, did I so surely protect you. For if you were to fall, and die, I would come with you, and into that fabulous kingdom we would pass together, my coat laid over you, my sperm still alive in your warm turns. Two struggling horses pulled us, swaying, up the still black hill of air northward. Oblivious, you were mine. I loved the oval of starlight that described your face. I loved the chill that brought your head to my shoulder. I loved the household labour that had left your knuckles rough, and the youth that had left your forearms downy, and the way you were lost in the shape of my coat.

Then I left you. The engines roared in a graver key, Manhattan bristled, the ocean lifted to swallow us, the wheels smacked the runway, our moment passed, we did not die. I hated our failure to die. I hated my haste in taking my coat from you and pulling my suitcase from under the seat and shoving down the aisle to be the first off. Ruth would be meeting me; it was after nine. I left you half asleep, pushing the hair back from your lips, abandoned, the prey of feeding eyes. I felt you watching me race, cowardly, across the cement, diminishing, flickering in the whirling lights. Already I had seen Ruth's face waiting in the anxious crowd behind the glass doors. I felt myself disappear in your eyes. I embraced her.

When the telephone rang the next morning at ten, Josie blushed angrily and left the kitchen. Sally answered it in her bathing suit; Peter had been waiting to go to the beach for half an hour. 'Hi,' she said. If it were someone else calling, her tone of voice would seem a joke.

'Hi,' Harry said. 'What happened?'

'Nothing,' Sally said. 'I got home around eleven and he was in bed asleep. This morning, before the train, he asked how the Fitches were, and I said fine, and that was all we said.'

'You're kidding. He must know something.'

'I don't think so, Harry. I just think we've got to such a point he doesn't really care what I do.'

'No. He cares.'

'How did it go with Ruth?'

'Fine. The plane mix-up gave me something to talk about, leaving you out, of course. I told her about the rent-a-car girls and Fancher and Wigglesworth. It made me sort of sad, how happy she was to see me. She was about to give up hope.'

Sunlight lay sharply on the salt and pepper shakers on the windowsill. Sally wondered vaguely if the salt would melt. 'I saw her meet you,' she said.

'Did you? I wasn't sure how much you could see.'

'The way you hustled her out of the waiting room, it looked as if you were carrying her.'

He laughed. 'Yes, she said, "What's the rush?" She's actually kind of depressed. Geoffrey broke his collar-bone while I was away, and Aunt Paula is coming for the week-end.'

'My God, Harry. His collar-bone?'

'Apparently it's not as serious as it sounds. Charlie pushed him down on the grass and he cried all day and held his arm funny, so she took him to the hospital and all they did was wrap an Ace bandage around his shoulders, to hold it back. Now he walks around like a little old man and doesn't want you to touch him.'

Peter came into the kitchen and began bumping, infuriatingly, against her bare legs. 'I'm sorry,' she said.

'Don't be. You didn't do it. Hey?'

'Yes?'

'You were lovely. Just killingly lovely.'

'So were you. It was even nicer than the first time.'

'I felt rotten about the ordeal in the airport. I'm amazed you survived it.'

'I didn't mind it, Harry. It was fun.'

'You're great. You're really so great, Sally, I just don't know what to do with you. You were so beautiful in the plane back, I'm all upset.'

'I felt badly about falling asleep. It's such a waste of my time with you.'

'No. It's not a waste. It was right.'

'I really was feeling quite weak. You make me weak, Harry.

'Hey. Was it really all right? Are you sorry you came?'

'Of course not.'

'It was sort of a sad lunch in the museum, and then the business about the toys was very sad.'

'I'm sorry about that. I wish I were a bigger person. I'm just not big enough to be your cheerful broad.'

'Listen – '

'And you make me feel terribly guilty about Geoffrey's collar-bone.'

'Why? Don't. It has nothing to do with you.'

'Yes it does. It's the sort of thing I make happen. I'm bad luck. I'm destroying Richard, and my children, and your children, and Ruth – ' Her eyes smarted and she wondered again if the salt in the sunstruck salt-cellar was melting.

'No, listen. You're not. It's me. I'm the man, and you're the woman, and it's up to me to control this, and I can't. You're good. You must know you're great; but do you know that you're good?'

'Sometimes when you tell me I feel it.'

'Good. Right. Do.'

Peter began plucking at her dangling arm, and his voice

began to grind. '*Go*, Mom. *Go-o*.' His soft, plucking body was jogging in exasperation.

She told Harry, 'Peter's being horrible and Josie is throwing one of her fits in the living room so I'd better hang up.'

'Sure. In a moment I have to tell the big cheese what I learned in Washington about the Third World. I'm sorry about Josie. If we get married, must we keep her?'

'We aren't going to get married, Harry.'

'Don't say that. I live by thinking that somehow we will. Are you sure we won't?'

He wanted to know, he wanted to be told she was sure. 'Not always,' she said.

He paused, and then said, 'Good.'

'I'll be appreciating all day tomorrow, so don't call me until Friday. I think we should take it easy now for a while, so I don't know when I'll see you again.'

'Yes. I suppose we shouldn't press our luck.'

She had hoped he would argue, and set a day soon. '*Peter*,' she snapped. 'Shall Mommy smack you?'

'Don't be cross with Peter,' Harry's voice said in her ear. 'He worries about you.'

'I must hang up. Good-bye?'

'Good-bye. I love you. Don't be too lovely for anybody else.'

'Have a good day, Harry.' She hung up, quickly, for she knew they could go on and on, and she would never tire of hearing his voice say things she doubted he believed. *Don't be too lovely for anybody else* – this was a favourite concept of his, that she would take on another man. He thought she was a tramp; she experienced a flash of hating him, and stood there, desperate, beautiful in her bathing suit, her naked feet caught in a warm slant of sun. Was she wicked or crazy? How could she possibly take this man away from his blameless wife and helpless children? Though Peter was frantic, she stood a moment longer, waiting to be told how.

John Updike

Bech in Romania

Henry Bech, the moderately well-known American author, was travelling in the countries of Eastern Europe as a cultural delegate. Deplaning in Bucharest wearing an astrakhan hat purchased in Moscow, he was not recognized by the United States Embassy personnel sent to greet him, and, rather than identify himself, sat sullenly on a bench, glowering like a Ukrainian machinery exporter, while these young men ran back and forth conversing with each other in dismayed English and shouting at the customs officials in what Bech took to be pidgin Romanian. At last, one of these young men, the smallest and cleverest, Princeton '51 or so, noticing the rounded toes of Bech's American shoes, ventured suspiciously, 'I beg your pardon, *pazhalusta*, but are you – ?'

'It's possible,' Bech said. After five weeks of consorting with Communists, he felt himself increasingly tempted to evade, confuse, and mock his compatriots. Further, after attuning himself to the platitudinous jog of translatorese, he found rapid English idiom exhausting. So it was with some relief that he passed, in the next hours, from the conspiratorial company of the Americans into the care of a monarchical Romanian hotel and a smiling Party underling called Athanase Petrescu.

Petrescu, whose oval face was adorned by constant sunglasses and several round sticking plasters placed upon a fresh blue shave, had translated into Romanian *Typee,*

Pierre, Life on the Mississippi, Sister Carrie, Winesburg, Ohio, Across the River and Into the Trees, and *On the Road.* He knew Bech's work well and said, 'Although it was *Travel Light* that made your name illustrious, yet in my heart I detect a very soft spot for *Brother Pig,* which your critics did not so much applaud.'

Bech recognized in Petrescu, behind the blue jaw and sinister glasses, a man humbly in love with books, a fool for literature. As, that afternoon, they strolled through a strange Bucharest park containing bronze busts of Goethe and Pushkin and Victor Hugo, beside a lake wherein the greenish sunset was coated with silver, the translator talked excitedly of a dozen things, sharing thoughts he had not been able to share while descending, alone at his desk, into the luminous abysses and profound crudities of American literature. 'With Hemingway, the difficulty of translating – and I speak to an extent of Anderson also – is to prevent the simplicity from seeming simple-minded. For we do not have here such a tradition of belle-lettrist fancifulness against which the style of Hemingway was a rebel. Do you follow the difficulty?'

'Yes. How did you get around it?'

Petrescu did not seem to understand. 'Get around, how? Circumvent?'

'How did you translate the simple language without seeming simple-minded?'

'Oh. By being extremely subtle.'

'Oh. I should tell you, some people in my country think Hemingway *was* simple-minded. It is actively debated.'

Petrescu absorbed this with a nod, and said, 'I know for a fact, his Italian is not always correct.'

When Bech got back to his hotel – situated on a square rimmed with buildings made, it seemed, of dusty pink candy – a message had been left for him to call Phillips at the U.S. Embassy. Phillips was Princeton '51. He asked, 'What have they got mapped out for you?'

Bech's schedule had hardly been discussed. 'Petrescu mentioned a production of *Desire Under the Elms* I might see. And he wants to take me to Braşov. Where is Braşov?'

'In Transylvania, way the hell off. It's where Dracula hung out. Listen, can we talk frankly?'

'We can try.'

'I know damn well this line is bugged, but here goes. This country is hot. Anti-Socialism is bursting out all over. My inkling is they want to get you out of Bucharest, away from all the liberal writers who are dying to meet you.'

'Are you sure they're not dying to meet Arthur Miller?'

'Kidding aside, Bech, there's a lot of ferment in this country, and we want to plug you in. Now, when are you meeting Taru?'

'Knock knock. Taru. Taru Who?'

'Jesus, he's the head of the Writers' Union – hasn't Petrescu even set up an appointment? Boy, they're putting you right around the old mulberry bush. I gave Petrescu a list of writers for you to latch on to. Suppose I call him and wave the big stick and ring you back. Got it?'

'Got it, tiger.' Bech hung up sadly; one of the reasons he had accepted the State Department's invitation was that he thought it would be an escape from agents.

Within ten minutes his phone rasped, in that dead rattly way it has behind the Iron Curtain, and it was Phillips, breathless, victorious. 'Congratulate me,' he said. 'I've been making like a thug and got *their* thugs to give you an appointment with Taru tonight.'

'This very night?'

Phillips sounded hurt. 'You're only here four nights, you know. Petrescu will pick you up. His excuse was he thought you might want some rest.'

'He's extremely subtle.'

'What was that?'

'Never mind, *pazhalusta*.'

Petrescu came for Bech in a black car driven by a hunched silhouette. The Writers' Union was housed on the other side of town, in a kind of castle, a turreted mansion with a flaring stone staircase and an oak-vaulted library whose shelves were twenty feet high and solid with leather spines. The stairs and chambers seemed deserted. Petrescu tapped on a tall panelled door of blackish oak, strap-hinged in the sombre Spanish style. The door soundlessly opened, revealing a narrow high room hung with tapestries, pale brown and blue, whose subject involved masses of attenuated soldiery unfathomably engaged. Behind a huge polished desk quite bare of furnishings sat an immaculate miniature man with a pink face and hair as white as a dandelion poll. His rosy hands, perfectly finished down to each fingernail, were folded on the shiny desk, reflected like water flowers; and his face wore a smiling expression that was also, in each neat crease, beyond improvement. This was Taru.

He spoke with magical suddenness, like a music box. Petrescu translated his words to Bech as 'You are a literary man. Do you know the works of our Mihail Sadoveanu, of our noble Mihail Beniuc, or perhaps that most wonderful spokesman for the people, Tudor Arghezi?'

Bech said, 'No, I'm afraid the only Romanian writer I know at all is Ionesco.'

The exquisite white-haired man nodded eagerly and emitted a length of tinkling sounds that was translated to Bech as simply 'And who is he?'

Petrescu, who certainly knew all about Ionesco, stared at Bech with blank expectance. Even in this innermost sanctum he had kept his sun-glasses on. Bech said, irritated, 'A playwright. Lives in Paris. Theatre of the Absurd. Wrote *Rhinoceros*,' and he crooked a forefinger beside his heavy Jewish nose, to represent a horn.

Taru emitted a dainty sneeze of laughter, Petrescu translated, listened, and told Bech, 'He is very sorry he has not heard of this man. Western books are a luxury here, so we are not able to follow each new nihilist movement. Comrade Taru asks what you plan to do while in the People's Republic of Romania.'

'I am told,' Bech said, 'that there are some writers interested in exchanging ideas with an American colleague. I believe my embassy has suggested a list to you.'

The musical voice went on and on. Petrescu listened with a cocked ear and relayed, 'Comrade Taru sincerely wishes that this may be the case and regrets that, because of the lateness of the hour and the haste of this meeting urged by your embassy, no secretaries are present to locate this list. He furthermore regrets that at this time of the year so many of our fine writers are bathing at the Black Sea. However, he points out that there is an excellent production of *Desire Under the Elms* in Bucharest, and that our Carpathian city of Braşov is indeed worthy of a visit. Comrade Taru himself retains many pleasant youthful memories concerning Braşov.'

Taru rose to his feet – an intensely dramatic event within the reduced scale he had established around himself. He spoke, thumped his small square chest resoundingly, spoke again, and smiled. Petrescu said, 'He wishes you to know that in his youth he published many books of poetry, both epic and lyric in manner. He adds, "A fire ignited here" ' – and here Petrescu struck his own chest in flaccid mimicry – ' "can never be quenched".'

Bech stood and responded, 'In my country we also ignite fires *here*.' He touched his head. His remark was not translated and, after an efflorescent display of courtesy from the brilliant-haired little man, Bech and Petrescu made their way through the empty mansion down to the waiting car, which drove them, rather jerkily, back to the hotel.

'And how did you like Mr Taru?' Petrescu asked on the way.

'He's a doll,' Bech said.

'You mean – a puppet?'

Bech turned curiously but saw nothing in Petrescu's face that betrayed more than a puzzlement over meaning. Bech said, 'I'm sure you have a better eye for the string than I do.'

Since neither had eaten, they dined together at the hotel;

they discussed Faulkner and Hawthorne while waiters brought them soup and veal a continent removed from the cabbagy cuisine of Russia. A lithe young woman on awkwardly high heels stalked among the tables singing popular songs from Italy and France. The trailing microphone wire now and then became entangled in her feet, and Bech admired the sly savagery with which she would, while not altering an iota her enamelled smile, kick herself free. Bech had been a long time without a woman. He looked forward to three more nights sitting at this table, surrounded by travelling salesmen from East Germany and Hungary, feasting on the sight of this lithe chanteuse. Though her motions were angular and her smile was inflexible, her high round bosom looked soft as a soufflé.

But tomorrow, Petrescu explained, smiling sweetly beneath his sad-eyed sun-glasses, they would go to Braşov.

Bech knew little about Romania. From his official briefing he knew it was 'a Latin island in a Slavic sea', that during the Second World War its anti-Semitism had been the most ferocious in Europe, that now it was seeking economic independence of the Soviet bloc. The ferocity especially interested him, since of the many human conditions it was his business to imagine, murderousness was among the most difficult. He was a Jew. Though he could be irritable and even vengeful, obstinate savagery was excluded from his budget of emotions.

Petrescu met him in the hotel lobby at nine and, taking his suitcase from his hand, led him to the hired car. By daylight, the driver was a short man the colour of ashes – white ash for the face, grey cigarette ash for his close-trimmed smudge of a moustache, and the darker residue of a tougher substance for his eyes and hair. His manner was nervous and remote and fussy; Bech's impression was of a stupidity so severe that the mind is tensed to sustain the simplest tasks. As they drove from the city, the driver constantly tapped his horn to warn pedestrians and cyclists of his approach. They passed the pre-war stucco suburbs, suggestive of southern California; the post-war Moscow-style apartment buildings, rectilinear and airless; the heretical all-glass exposition hall the Romanians had built to celebrate twenty years of industrial progress under Socialism. It was shaped like a huge sailor's cap, and before it stood a tall Brancusi column cast in aluminium.

'Brancusi,' Bech said. 'I didn't know you acknowledged him.'

'Oh, much,' Petrescu said. 'his village is a shrine. I can show you many early works in our national museum.'

'And Ionesco? Is he really a non-person?'

Petrescu smiled. 'The eminent head of our Writers' Union,' he said, 'makes little jokes. He is known here but not much produced as yet. Students in their rooms perhaps read about a play like *The Singer Without Hair.*'

Bech was distracted from the conversation by the driver's incessant mutter of tooting. They were in the country now, driving along a straight, slightly rising road lined with trees whose trunks were painted white. On the shoulder of the road walked bundle-shaped old women carrying knotted bundles, little boys tapping donkeys forward, men in French-blue work clothes sauntering empty-handed. At all of them the driver sounded his horn. His stubby, grey-nailed hand fluttered on the contact rim, producing an agitated stammer beginning perhaps a hundred yards in advance and continuing until the person, who usually moved only to turn and scowl, had been passed. Since the road was well travelled, the noise was practically uninterrupted, and after the first half hour nagged Bech like a toothache. He asked Petrescu, 'Must he do that?'

'Oh, yes. He is a conscientious man.'

'What good does it do?'

Petrescu, who had been developing an exciting thought on Mark Twain's infatuation with the apparatus of capitalism, which had undermined his bucolic genius, indulgently explained, 'The bureau from which we hire cars provides the driver. They have been precisely trained for this profession.'

Bech realized that Petrescu himself did not drive. He reposed in the oblivious trust of an airplane passenger, legs crossed, sunglasses in place, issuing smoother and smoother phrases, while Bech leaned forward desperately, braking on the empty floor, twitching a wheel that was not there, trying to wrench the car's control away from this atrociously unrhythmic and brutal driver. When they went through a village, the driver would speed up and intensify the mutter of his honking; clusters of peasants and geese exploded in disbelief, and Bech felt as if gears, the gears that space and engage the mind, were clashing. As they ascended into the mountains, the driver demonstrated his technique with curves: he approached each like an enemy, accelerating, and at the last moment stepped on the brake as if crushing something underfoot. In the jerking and swaying, Petrescu grew pale. His blue jaw acquired a moist sheen and issued phrases less smoothly. Bech said to him, 'This driver should be locked up. He is sick and dangerous.'

'No, no, he is a good man. These roads, they are difficult.'

'At least please ask him to stop twiddling the horn. It's torture.'

Petrescu's eyebrows arched, but he leaned forward and spoke in Romanian.

The driver answered; the language clattered in his mouth, though his voice was soft.

Petrescu told Bech, 'He says it is a safety precaution.'

'Oh, for Christ's sake!'

Petrescu was truly puzzled. He asked, 'In the States, you drive your own car?'

'Of course, everybody does,' Bech said, and then worried that he had hurt the feelings of this Socialist, who must submit to the aristocratic discomfort of being driven. For the remainder of the trip, he held silent about the driver. The muddy lowland fields with Mediterranean farmhouses had yielded to fir-dark hills bearing Germanic chalets. At the highest point, the old boundary of Austria-Hungary, fresh snow had fallen, and the car, pressed ruthlessly through the ruts, brushed within inches of some children dragging sleds. It was a short downhill distance from there to Braşov. They stopped before a newly built pistachio hotel. The jarring ride had left Bech with a headache. Petrescu stepped carefully from the car, licking his lips; the tip of his tongue showed purple in his drained face. The driver, as composed as raked ashes no touch of wind has stirred, changed out of his grey driving coat, checked the oil and water, and removed his lunch from the trunk. Bech examined him for some sign of satisfaction, some betraying trace of malice, but there was nothing. His eyes were living smudges, and his mouth was the mouth of the boy in the class, who, being neither strong nor intelligent, has developed insignificance into a positive character trait that does him some credit. He glanced at Bech without feeling; yet Bech suddenly wondered if the man did not understand a little English.

In Braşov the American writer and his escort passed the time in harmless sightseeing. The local museum contained peasant costumes. The local castle contained armour. The Lutheran cathedral was surprising; Gothic lines and scale had been wedded to clear glass and an austerity of decoration, noble and mournful, that left one, Bech felt, much too alone with God. He felt the Reformation here as a desolating wind, four hundred years ago. From the hotel roof, the view looked sepia, and there was an empty swimming pool, and wet snow on the lacy metal chairs. Petrescu shivered and went down to his room. Bech changed neckties and went down to the bar. Chubby Checker bubbled from the walls. The bartender understood what a Martini was, though he used equal parts of gin and vermouth. The clientele was young, and many spoke Hungarian, for Transylvania had been taken from Hungary after the war. One plausible youth, working with Bech's reluctant French, elicited from him that he was *un écrivain*, and asked for his autograph. But this turned out to be the prelude to a proposed exchange of pens, in which Bech lost a sentimentally cherished Esterbrook and gained a nameless ballpoint that wrote red. Bech wrote three and a half postcards (to his mistress, his mother, his publisher, and a half to his editor at *Commentary*) before the red pen went dry. Petrescu, who neither drank nor smoked, finally appeared. Bech said, 'My hero, where have you been? I've had four Martinis and been swindled in your absence.'

Petrescu was embarrassed. 'I've been shaving.'

'Shaving!'

'Yes, it is humiliating. I must spend each day one hour shaving, and even yet it does not look as if I have shaved, my beard is so obdurate.'

'Are you putting blades in the razor?'

'Oh, yes, I buy the best and use two upon each occasion.'

'This is the saddest story I've ever heard. Let me send you some decent blades when I get home.'

'Please, do not. There are no blades better than the blades I use. It is merely that my beard is phenomenal.'

'When you die,' Bech said, 'you can leave it to Romanian science.'

'You are ironical.'

In the restaurant, there was dancing – the Tveest, the Hully Gullee, and chain formations that involved a lot of droll hopping. American dances had become here innocently bird-like. Now and then a young man, slender and with hair combed into a parrot's peak, would leap into the air and seem to hover, emitting a shrill palatal cry. The men in Romania appeared lighter and more fanciful than the women, who moved, in their bell-skirted cocktail dresses, with a wooden stateliness perhaps inherited from their peasant grandmothers. Each girl who passed near their table was described by Petrescu, not humorously at first, as a 'typical Romanian beauty'.

'And this one, with the orange lips and eyelashes?'

'A typical Romanian beauty. The cheekbones are very classical.'

'And the blonde behind her? The small plump one?'

'Also typical.'

'But they are so different. Which is more typical?'

'They are equally. We are a perfect democracy.' Between spates of dancing, a young chanteuse, more talented than the one in the Bucharest hotel, with curlier hair and a bouncier manner, took the floor with a microphone. She had learned, probably from free-world films, that terrible mannerism of strenuousness whereby every note, no matter how accessibly placed and how flatly attacked, is given a facial aura of immense accomplishment. Her smile, at the close of each number, triumphantly combined a conspiratorial twinkle, a sublime humility, and the dazed self-congratulation of post-coital euphoria. Yet, beneath the artifice, the girl had life. Bech was enchanted by a number, in Italian, that involved much animated pouting and finger-scolding and placing of the fists on the hips. Petrescu explained that the song was the plaint of a young wife whose husband was always attending soccer matches and never stayed at home with her. Bech asked, 'Is she also a typical Romanian beauty?'

'I think,' Petrescu said, with a purr Bech had not heard before, 'she is a typical little Jewess.'

The drive, late the next afternoon, back to Bucharest was worse than the one out, for it took place partly in the dark. The driver met the challenge with increased speed and redoubled honking. In a rare intermittence of danger, a straight road near Ploesi where only the oil rigs relieved the flatness, Bech asked, 'Seriously, do you not feel the insanity of this man?' Five minutes before, the driver had turned to the back seat and, showing even grey teeth in a tight tic of a smile, had remarked about a dog lying dead beside the road. Bech suspected that most of the remark had not been translated.

Petrescu said, crossing his legs in the effete and weary

way that had begun to exasperate Bech, 'No, he is a good man, an extremely kind man, who takes his work too seriously. In that he is like the beautiful Jewess whom you so much admired.'

'In my country,' Bech said, ' "Jewess" is a kind of fighting word.'

'Here,' Petrescu said, 'it is merely descriptive. Let us talk about Herman Melville. Is it possible to you that *Pierre* is a yet greater work than *The White Whale*?'

'No, I think it is yet not so great, possibly.'

'You are ironical about my English. Please excuse it. Being prone to motion sickness has discollected my thoughts.'

'Our driver would discollect anybody's thoughts. Is it possible that he is the late Adolf Hitler, kept alive by Count Dracula?'

'I think not. Our people's uprising in 1944 fortunately exterminated the Fascists.'

'That is fortunate. Have you ever read, speaking of Melville, *Omoo*?'

Melville, it happened, was Bech's favourite American author, in whom he felt united the strengths that were later to go the separate ways of Dreiser and James. Throughout dinner, back at the hotel, he lectured Petrescu about him. 'No one,' Bech said – he had ordered a full bottle of white Romanian wine, and his tongue felt agile as a butterfly – 'more courageously faced our native terror. He went for it right between its wide-set little pig eyes, and it shattered his genius like a lance.' He poured himself more wine. The hotel chanteuse, who Bech now noticed had buck teeth as well as gawky legs, stalked to their table, untangled her feet from the microphone wire, and favoured them with a French version of 'Some Enchanted Evening'.

'You do not consider,' Petrescu said, 'that Hawthorne also went between the eyes? And the laconic Ambrose Bierce?'

'*Quelque soir enchanté*,' the girl sang, her eyes and teeth and earrings glittering like the facets of a chandelier.

'Hawthorne blinked,' Bech said, 'and Bierce squinted.'

'*Vous verrez l'étranger . . .*'

'I worry about you, Petrescu,' Bech continued. 'Don't you ever have to go home? Isn't there a Frau Petrescu, Madame, or whatever, a typical Romanian, never mind.' Abruptly he felt steeply lonely.

In bed, when his room had stopped the gentle swaying motion with which it had greeted his entrance, he remembered the driver, and the man's neatly combed death-grey face seemed the face of everything foul, stale, stupid, and uncontrollable in the world. He had seen that tight tic of a smile before. Where? He remembered. West Eighty-sixth Street, coming back from Riverside Park, a childhood playmate, with whom he always argued, and was always right, and always lost. Their ugliest quarrel had concerned comic strips, whether or not the artist – Segar, say, who drew Popeye, or Harold Gray of Little Orphan Annie – whether or not the artist, in duplicating the faces from panel to panel, day after day, traced them. Bech had maintained, obviously, not. The other boy had insisted that some mechanical process was used. Bech tried to explain that it was not such a difficult feat, that just as one's handwriting is always the same, so – The other boy, his face clouding, said it wasn't possible. Bech explained, what he felt so clearly, that everything was possible for human beings, with a little training and talent, that the ease and variation of each panel proved – The other face had become totally closed, with a density quite inhuman, as it steadily shook 'No, no, no,' and Bech, becoming frightened and furious, tried to behead the other boy with his fists, and the boy in turn pinned him and pressed his face into the bitter grits of pebble and glass that coated the cement passageway between two apartment buildings. These unswept jagged bits, a kind of city topsoil, had enlarged under his eyes, and this experience, the magnification amidst pain of those negligible mineral flecks, had formed, perhaps, a vision. At any rate, it seemed to Bech, as he skidded into sleep, that his artistic gifts had been squandered in the attempt to recapture that moment of abrasive precision.

The next day, his last full day in Romania, Petrescu took him to an art museum where, amid many ethnic posters posing as paintings, a few sketches and sculpted heads by the young Brancusi smelled like saints' bones. The two men went on to the twenty years' industrial exhibit and admired rows of brightly painted machinery – counters in some large international game. They visited shops, and everywhere Bech felt a desiccated pinkish elegance groping, out of eclipse, through the murky hardware of Sovietism, towards a rebirth of style. Yet there had been a tough and heroic naïveté in Russia that he missed here, where something shrugging and effete seemed to leave room for a vein of energetic evil. In the evening, they went to *Patima de Sub Ulmi.*

Their driver, bringing them to the very door of the theatre, pressed his car forward through bodies, up an arc of driveway crowded with pedestrians. The people caught in the headlights were astonished; Bech slammed his foot on a phantom brake and Petrescu grunted and strained backward in his seat. The driver continually tapped his horn – a demented, persistent muttering – and slowly the crowd gave way around the car. Bech and Petrescu stepped, at the door, into the humid atmosphere of a riot. As the chauffeur, his childish small-nosed profile impassive, pressed his car back through the crowd to the street, fists thumped on the fenders.

Safe in the theatre lobby, Petrescu took off his sunglasses to wipe his face. His eyes were a tender bulging blue, with jaundiced whites; a scholar's tremor pulsed in his left lower lid. 'You know,' he confided to Bech, 'that man our driver. Not all is well with him.'

'You're kidding,' Bech said.

O'Neill's starveling New England farmers were played as Russian muzhiks; they wore broad-belted coats and high black boots and kept walloping each other on the back.

Abbie Cabot had become a typical Romanian beauty, ten years past prime, with a beauty spot on one cheek and artful bare arms as supple as a swan's neck. Since their seats were in the centre of the second row, Bech had a good if infrequent view down the front of her dress, and thus, ignorant of when the plot would turn her his way, he contentedly manufactured suspense for himself. But Petrescu, his loyalty to American letters affronted beyond endurance, insisted that they leave after the first act. 'Wrong, wrong,' he complained. 'Even the pitchforks were wrong.'

'I'll have the State Department send them an authentic American pitchfork,' Bech promised.

'And the girl – the girl is not like that, not a coquette. She is a religious innocent, under economic stress.'

'Well, scratch an innocent, find a coquette.'

'It is your good nature to joke, but I am ashamed you saw such a travesty. Now our driver is not here. We are undone.'

The street outside the theatre, so recently jammed, was empty and dark. A solitary couple walked slowly towards them. With surrealist abruptness, Petrescu fell into the arms of the man, walloping his back, and then kissed the calmly proffered hand of the woman. The couple was introduced to Bech as 'a most brilliant young writer and his notably ravishing wife'. The man, stolid and forbidding, wore rimless glasses and a bulky checked topcoat. The woman was scrawny; her face, potentially handsome, had been worn to its bones by the nervous burden of intelligence. She had a cold and a command, quick but limited, of English. 'Are you having a liking for this?' she asked.

Bech understood her gesture to include all Romania. 'Very much,' he answered. 'After Russia, it seems very civilized.'

'And who isn't?' she said. 'What are you liking most?'

Petrescu roguishly interposed, 'He has a passion for nightclub singers.'

The wife translated this to her husband; he took his hands from his overcoat pockets and clapped them. He was wearing leather gloves, so the noise was loud on the deserted street. He spoke, and Petrescu translated, 'He says we should therefore, as hosts, escort you to the most celebrated night club in Bucharest, where you will see many singers, each more glorious than the preceding.'

'But,' Bech said, 'weren't they going somewhere? Shouldn't they go home?' It worried him that Communists never seemed to go home.

'For why?' the wife cried.

'You have a cold,' Bech told her. Her eyes didn't comprehend. He touched his own nose, so much larger than hers. '*Un rhume.*'

'Poh!' she said. 'Itself takes care of tomorrow.'

The writer owned a car, and he drove them, with the gentleness of a pedal boat, through a maze of alleys overhung by cornices suggestive of cake frosting, of waves breaking, of seashells, lion paws, unicorn horns, and cumulus clouds. They parked across the street from a blue sign, and went into a green doorway, and down a yellow set of stairs. Music approached them from one direction and a coat-check girl in net tights from the other. It was to Bech as if he were dreaming of an American night club, giving it the strange spaciousness of dreams. The main room had been conjured out of several basements – a cave hollowed from the underside of jewellers' shops and vegetable marts. Tables were set in shadowy tiers arranged around a central square floor. Here a man with a red wig and mascaraed eyes was talking into a microphone, mincingly. Then he sang, in the voice of a choirboy castrated too late. A waiter materialized. Bech ordered Scotch, the other writer ordered vodka. The wife asked for cognac and Petrescu for mineral water. Three girls dressed as rather naked bicyclists appeared with a dwarf on a unicycle and did some unsmiling gyrations to music while he pedalled among them, tugging bows and displacing straps. 'Typical Polish beauties,' Petrescu explained in Bech's ear. He and the writer's wife were seated on the tier behind Bech. Two women, one a girl in her teens and the other a heavy old blonde, perhaps her mother, both dressed identically in sequinned silver, did a hypnotic, languorous act with tinted pigeons, throwing them up in the air, watching them wheel through the shadows of the night club, and holding out their wrists for their return. They juggled with the pigeons, passed them between their legs, and for a climax the elderly blonde fed an aquamarine pigeon with seeds held in her mouth and fetched, one by one, on to her lips. 'Czechs,' Petrescu explained. The master of ceremonies reappeared in a blue wig and a toreador's jacket, and did a comic act with the dwarf, who had been fitted with papier-mâché horns. An East German girl, flaxen-haired and apple-cheeked, with the smooth columnar legs of the very young, came to the microphone dressed in a brief parody of a cowgirl outfit and sang, in English, 'Dip in the Hot of Texas' and 'Allo Cindy Lou, Goot-bye Hot'. She pulled guns from her hips and received much pro-American applause, but Bech was on his third Scotch and needed his hand to hold cigarettes. The Romanian writer sat at the table beside him, a carafe of vodka at his elbow, staring stolidly at the floor show. He looked like the young Theodore Roosevelt, or perhaps McGeorge Bundy. His wife leaned forward and said in Bech's ear, 'Is just like home, hey? Texas is ringing bells?' He decided she was being sarcastic. A fat man in a baggy maroon tuxedo set up a long table and kept eight tin plates twirling on the ends of flexible sticks. Bech thought it was miraculous, but the man was booed. A touching black-haired girl from Bulgaria hesitantly sang three atonal folk songs into a chastened silence. Three women behind Bech began to chatter hissingly. Bech turned to rebuke them and was stunned by the size of their wristwatches, which were man-sized, as in Russia. Also, in turning he had surprised Petrescu and the writer's wife holding hands. Though it was after midnight, the customers were still coming in, and the floor show refused to stop. The Polish girls returned dressed as ponies and jumped through the hoops the dwarf held for them. The master of ceremonies reappeared in a striped bathing suit and black wig and did an act with the dwarf involving a step-ladder and a bucket of water. A black dancer from Ghana twirled firebrands in the dark while slapping the floor with her bare feet. Four Latvian tumblers performed on a trampoline and a see-saw. The Czech mother and daughter came back in different costumes, spangled gold, but performed the identical act, the pigeons whirring, circling, returning, eating from the mother's lips. Then five Chinese girls from Outer Mongolia –

'My God,' Bech said, 'isn't this ever going to be over?'

The writer's wife told him, 'For your money, you really gets.'

Petrescu and she conferred and decided it was time to go. One of the big wrist watches behind Bech said two o'clock. In leaving, they had to pass around the Chinese girls, who, each clad in a snug beige bikini, were concealing and revealing their bodies amid a weave of rippling coloured flags. One of the girls glanced sideways at Bech, and he blew her a pert kiss, as if from a train window. Their yellow bodies looked fragile to him; he felt that their bones, like the bones of birds, had evolved hollow, to save weight. At the mouth of the cave, the effeminate master of ceremonies, wearing a parrot headdress, was conferring with the hat-check girl. His intent was plainly heterosexual; Bech's head reeled at such duplicity. Though they added the weight of his coat to him, he rose like a balloon up the yellow stairs, bumped out through the green door, and stood beneath the blue light inhaling volumes of the cool Romanian night.

He felt duty-bound to confront the other writer. They stood, the two of them, on the cobbled pavement, as if on opposite sides of a transparent wall one side of which was coated with Scotch and the other with vodka. The other's rimless glasses were misted and the resemblance to Teddy Roosevelt had been dissipated. Bech asked him, 'What do you write about?'

The wife, patting her nose with a handkerchief and struggling not to cough, translated the question, and the answer, which was brief. 'Peasants,' she told Bech. 'He wants to know, what do *you* write about?'

Bech spoke to him directly. '*La bourgeoisie*,' he said; and that completed the cultural exchange. Gently bumping and rocking, the writer's car took Bech back to his hotel, where he fell into the deep, unapologetic sleep of the sated.

The plane to Sofia left Bucharest the next morning. Petrescu and the ashen-faced driver came into the tall *fin-de-siècle* dining room for Bech while he was still eating breakfast – a finely seasoned omelette. Petrescu explained that the driver had gone back to the theatre, and waited until the ushers and the managers left, after midnight. But the driver did not seem resentful, and gave Bech, in the sallow morning light, a fractional smile, a *risus sardonicus*, in which his eyes did not participate. On the way to the airport, he scattered a flock of chickens an old woman was coaxing across the road, and forced a military transport truck on to the shoulder, while its load of soldiers gestured and jeered. Bech's stomach grovelled, bathing his breakfast in acid. The ceaseless tapping of the horn seemed a gnawing on all of his nerve ends. Petrescu made a fastidious mouth and sighed through his nostrils. 'I regret,' he said, 'that we did not make more occasion to discuss your exciting contemporaries.'

'I never read them. They're too exciting,' Bech said, as a line of uniformed schoolchildren was narrowly missed, and a fieldworker with a wheel-barrow shuffled to safety, spilling potatoes. The day was overcast above the loamy sunken fields and the roadside trees in their skirts of white paint. 'Why,' he asked, not having meant to be rude, 'are all these tree trunks painted?'

'So they are,' Petrescu said. 'I have not noticed this before, in all my years. Presumably it is a measure to defeat the insects.'

The driver spoke in Romanian, and Petrescu told Bech, 'He says it is for the car headlights, at night. Always he is thinking about his job.'

At the airport, all the Americans were there who had tried to meet Bech four days ago. Petrescu immediately delivered to Phillips, like a bribe, the name of the writer they had met last night, and Phillips said to Bech, 'You spent the evening with *him*? That's fabulous. He's the top of the list, man. We've never laid a finger on him before; he's been inaccessible.'

'Stocky guy with glasses?' Bech asked, shielding his eyes. Phillips was so pleased it was like a bright light too early in the day.

'That's the boy. For our money he's the hottest Red writer this side of Yevtushenko. He's *waaay* out. Stream of consciousness, no punctuation, everything. There's even some sex.'

'You might say he's Red hot,' Bech said.

'Huh? Yeah, that's good. Seriously, what did he say to you?'

'He said he'll defect to the West as soon as his shirts come back from the laundry.'

'And we went,' Petrescu said, 'to La Caverne Bleue.'

'Say,' Phillips said, 'you really went underground.'

'I think of myself,' Bech said modestly, 'as a sort of low-flying U-2.'

'All kidding aside, Henry' – and here Phillips took Bech by the arms and squeezed – 'it sounds as if you've done a sensational job for us. Sensational. Thanks, friend.'

Bech hugged everyone in parting – Phillips, the chargé d'affaires, the junior chargé d'affaires, the ambassador's twelve-year-old nephew, who was taking archery lessons near the airport and had to be dropped off. Bech saved Petrescu for last, and walloped his back, for the man had led him to remember what he was tempted to forget in America, that reading can be the best part of a man's life.

'I'll send you razor blades,' he promised, for in the embrace Petrescu's beard had scratched.

'No, no, I already buy the best. Send me books, any books!'

The plane was roaring to go, and only when safely, or fatally, sealed inside did Bech remember the driver. In the flurry of formalities and baggage handling there had been no good-bye. Worse, there had been no tip. The leu notes Bech had set aside were still folded in his wallet, and his start of guilt gave way, as the runways and dark fields tilted and dwindled under him, to a vengeful satisfaction and glad sense of release. Clouds blotted out the country. He realized that for four days he had been afraid. The man next to him, a portly Slav whose bald brow was beaded with apprehensive sweat, turned and confided something unintelligible, and Bech said, '*Pardon, je ne comprends pas. Je suis Américain.*'

John Updike

Man and Daughter in the Cold

'Look at that girl ski!' The exclamation arose at Ethan's side as if, in the disconnecting cold, a rib of his had cried out; but it was his friend, friend and fellow-teacher, an inferior teacher but superior skier, Matt Langley, admiring Becky, Ethan's own daughter. It took an effort, in this air like slices of transparent metal interposed everywhere, to make these connexions and to relate the young girl, her round face red with windburn as she skimmed down the run-out slope, to himself. She was his daughter, age thirteen. He had twin sons, two years younger, and his attention had always been focused on their skiing, on the irksome comedy of their double needs – the four boots to lace, the four mittens to find – and then their cute yet grim competition as now one and now the other gained the edge in the expertise of geländesprungs and slalom form. On their trips north into the mountains, Becky had come along for the ride. 'Look how solid she is,' Matt went on. 'She doesn't cheat on it like your boys – those feet are absolutely together.' The girl, grinning as if she could hear herself praised, wiggle-waggled to a flashy stop that sprayed snow over the men's ski tips.

'Where's Mommy?' she asked.

Ethan answered, 'She went with the boys into the lodge. They couldn't take it.' Their sinewy little male bodies had no insulation; weeping and shivering, they had begged to go in after a single T-bar run.

'What sissies,' Becky said.

Matt said, 'This wind is wicked. And it's picking up. You should have been here at nine; Lord, it was lovely. All that fresh powder, and not a stir of wind.'

Becky told him, 'Dumb Tommy couldn't find his mittens, we spent an *hour* looking, and then Daddy got the Jeep stuck.' Ethan, alerted now for signs of the wonderful in his daughter, was struck by the strange fact that she was making conversation. Unafraid, she was talking to Matt without her father's intercession.

'Mr Langley was saying how nicely you were skiing.'

'You're Olympic material, Becky.'

The girl perhaps blushed; but her cheeks could get no redder. Her eyes, which, were she a child, she would have instantly averted, remained a second on Matt's face, as if to estimate how much he meant it. 'It's easy down here,' Becky said. 'It's babyish.'

Ethan asked. 'Do you want to go up to the top?' He was freezing standing still, and the gondola would be shelter from the wind.

Her eyes shifted to his, with another unconsciously thoughtful hesitation. 'Sure. If you want to.'

'Come along, Matt?'

'Thanks, no. It's too rough for me; I've had enough runs. This is the trouble with January – once it stops snowing, the wind comes up. I'll keep Elaine company in the lodge.' Matt himself had no wife, no children. At thirty-eight, he was as free as his students, as light on his skis and as full of brave know-how. 'In case of frostbite,' he shouted after them, 'rub snow on it.'

Becky effortlessly skated ahead to the lift shed. The encumbered motion of walking on skis, not natural to him, made Ethan feel asthmatic: a fish out of water. He touched his parka pocket, to check that the inhalator was there. As a child he had imagined death as something attacking from outside, but now he saw that it was carried within; we nurse it for years, and it grows. The clock on the lodge wall said a quarter to noon. The giant thermometer read two degrees above zero. The racks outside were dense as hedges with idle skis. Crowds, any sensation of crowding or delay, quickened his asthma; as therapy he imagined the emptiness, the blue freedom, at the top of the mountain. The clatter of machinery inside the shed was comforting, and enough teenage boys were boarding gondolas to make the ascent seem normal and safe. Ethan's breathing eased. Becky proficiently handed her poles to the loader, points up; her father was always caught by surprise, and often as not fumbled the little manoeuvre of letting his skis be taken from him. Until, five years ago, he had become an assistant professor at a New Hampshire college an hour to the south, he had never skied; he had lived in those Middle Atlantic cities where snow, its moment of virgin beauty by, is only an encumbering nuisance, a threat of suffocation. Whereas his children had grown up on skis.

Alone with his daughter in the rumbling isolation of the gondola, he wanted to explore her, and found her strange – strange in her uninquisitive child's silence, her accustomed poise in this ascending egg of metal. A dark figure with spreading legs veered out of control beneath them, fell forward, and vanished. Ethan cried out, astonished, scandalized; he imagined the man had buried himself alive. Becky was barely amused, and looked away before the dark spots struggling in the drift were lost from sight. As if she might know, Ethan asked, 'Who was that?'

'Some kid.' Kids, her tone implied, were in plentiful supply; one could be spared.

He offered to dramatize the adventure ahead of them: 'Do you think we'll freeze at the top?'

'Not exactly.'

'What do you think it'll be like?'

'Miserable.'

'Why are we doing this, do you think?'

'Because we paid the money for the all-day lift ticket.'

'Becky, you think you're pretty smart, don't you?'

'Not really.'

The gondola rumbled and lurched into the shed at the top; an attendant opened the door, and there was a howling mixed of wind and of boys whooping to keep warm. He was roughly handed two pairs of skis, and the handler, muffled to the eyes with a scarf, stared as if astonished that Ethan was so old. All the others struggling into skis in the lee of the shed were adolescent boys: students. After fifteen years of teaching, Ethan tended to flinch from youth – its harsh noises, its cheerful rapacity, its cruel onward flow as one class replaced another, ate a year of his life, and was replaced by another.

Away from the shelter of the shed, the wind was a high monotonous pitch of pain. His cheeks instantly ached, and the hinges linking the elements of his face seemed exposed. His septum tingled like glass – the rim of a glass being rubbed by a moist finger to produce a note. Drifts ribbed the trail, obscuring Becky's ski tracks seconds after she made them, and at each push through the heaped snow his scope of breathing narrowed. By the time he reached the first steep section, the left half of his back hurt as it did only in the panic of a full asthmatic attack, and his skis, ignored, too heavy to manage, spread and swept him towards a snowbank at the side of the trail. He was bent far forward but kept his balance; the snow kissed his face lightly, instantly, all over; he straightened up, refreshed by the shock, thankful not to have lost a ski. Down the slope Becky had halted and was staring upward at him, worried. A huge blowing feather, a partition of snow, came between them. The cold, unprecedented in his experience, shone through his clothes like furious light, and as he rummaged through his parka for the inhalator he seemed to be searching glass shelves backed by a black wall. He found it, its icy plastic the touch of life, a clumsy key. Gasping, he exhaled, put it into his mouth, and inhaled; the isoproterenol spray, chilled into drops, opened his lungs enough for him to call to his daughter, 'Keep moving! I'll catch up!'

Becky's eyes and face hesitated, but she obeyed. Easily,

solid on her skis, she swung down among the moguls and wind-bared ice, and became small, and again waited. The moderate slope seemed a cliff; if he fell and sprained anything, he would freeze. His entire body would become solid, impermeable, locked tight against air and light and thought. His legs trembled; his breath moved in and out of a narrow slot beneath the pain in his back. The cold and blowing snow all around him constituted an immense crowding, but there was no way out of this white cave but to slide downward towards the dark spot that was his daughter. He had forgotten all his lessons. Leaning backward in an infant's tense snow plough, he floundered through layers of powder and ice.

'You O.K., Daddy?' Her stare was wide, its fright underlined by a pale patch on her right cheek.

He used the inhalator again and gave himself breath to tell her, 'I'm fine. Let's get down before I die.'

In this way, in steps of her leading and waiting, they worked down the mountain, out of the worst wind, into the lower trail that ran between birches and hemlocks. The cold had the quality not of absence but of force: an inverted burning. The last time Becky stopped and waited, the colourless crescent on her scarlet cheek disturbed him, reminded him of some injunction, but he could find in his brain, whittled to a dim determination to persist, only the advice to keep going, towards shelter and warmth. She told him, at a division of trails, 'This is the easier way.'

'Let's go the quicker way,' he said, and in this last descent recovered the rhythm – knees together, shoulders facing the valley, weight forward as if in the moment of release from a diving board – not a resistance but a joyous acceptance of falling. They reached the base lodge, and with unfeeling hands removed their skis. Pushing into the cafeteria, Ethan saw in the momentary mirror of the door window that his face was a spectre's; chin, nose, and eyebrows had retained the snow from that near-fall near the top.

'Becky, look,' he said, turning in the crowded warmth and clatter inside the door. 'I'm a monster.'

'I know, your face was all white, I didn't know whether to tell you or not. I thought it might scare you.'

He touched the pale patch on her cheek. 'Feel anything?'

'No.'

'Damn. I should have rubbed snow on it.'

Matt and Elaine and the twins, flushed and stripped of their parkas, had eaten lunch; shouting and laughing with a strange guilty shrillness, they said that there had been repeated loudspeaker announcements not to go up to the top without face masks, because of frost-bite. They had expected Ethan and Becky to come back down on the gondola, as others had, after tasting the top. 'It never occurred to us,' Ethan said. He took the blame upon himself by adding, 'I wanted to see the girl ski.'

Their common adventure, and the guilt of his having given her frost-bite, bound Becky and Ethan together in complicity for the rest of the day. They arrived home as light was leaving even the tips of the hills; Elaine had invited Matt to supper, and while the windows of the house burned golden Ethan shovelled out the Jeep. The house was a typical New Hampshire farmhouse, less than two miles from the college, on the side of a hill, overlooking what had been a pasture, with the usual capacious porch running around three sides, cluttered with cordwood and last summer's lawn furniture. The woodsy sheltered scent of these porches, the sense of rural waste space, never failed to please Ethan, who had been raised in a Newark half house, then a West Side apartment, and just before college a row house in Baltimore, with his grandparents. The wind had been left behind in the mountains. The air was as still as the stars. Shovelling the light dry snow became a lazy dance done without resistance. But when he bent suddenly, his knees creaked, and his breathing shortened so that he paused. A sudden rectangle of light was flung from the shadows of the porch. Becky came out into the cold with him. She was carrying a lawn rake.

He asked her, 'Should you be out again? How's your frost-bite?' Though she was a distance away, there was no need, in the immaculate air, to raise his voice.

'It's O.K. It kind of tingles. And under my chin. Mommy made me put on a scarf.'

'What's the lawn rake for?'

'It's a way you make a path. It really works.'

'O.K., you make a path to the garage and after I get my breath I'll see if I can get the Jeep back in.'

'Are you having asthma?'

'A little.'

'We were reading about it in biology. Dad, see, it's kind of a tree inside you, and every branch has a little ring of muscle around it, and they tighten.' From her gestures in the dark she was demonstrating, with mittens on.

What she described, of course, was classic unalloyed asthma, whereas his was shading into emphysema, which could only worsen. But he liked being lectured to – preferred it, indeed, to lecturing – and as the minutes of companionable silence with his daughter passed he took inward notes on the bright quick impressions flowing over him like a continuous voice. The silent cold. The stars. Orion behind an elm. Minute scintillae in the snow at his feet. His daughter's strange black bulk against the white; the solid grace that had stolen upon her. The conspiracy of love. His father and he shovelling the car free from a sudden unwelcome storm in Newark, instantly grey with soot, the undercurrent of desperation, his father a salesman and must get to Camden. Got to get to Camden, boy, get to Camden or bust. Dead of a heart attack at forty-seven. Ethan tossed a shovelful into the air so the scintillae flashed in the steady golden note from the house windows. Elaine and Matt sitting flushed at the lodge table, parkas off, in deshabille, as if sitting up in bed. Matt's way of turning a half circle on the top of a mogul, light as a diver. The cancerous unwieldiness of Ethan's own skis. His jealousy of his students, the many-headed immortality of their annual renewal. The flawless tall cruelty of the stars. Orion involved with the silhouetted elm. A black tree inside him. His daughter, busily sweeping with the rake, childish yet lithe, so curiously demonstrating this preference for his company. Feminine of her to forgive him for her frost-bite. Perhaps, flattered on skis, felt the cold her element. Her womanhood soon enough to be smothered in warmth. A plough a mile away painstakingly scraped. He was missing the point of the lecture. The point was unstated: an absence. He was looking upon his daughter as a woman but without lust. The music around him was being produced, in the zero air, like a finger on crystal, by this hollowness, this generosity of negation. Without lust, without jealousy. Space seemed love, bestowed to be free in, and coldness the price. He felt joined to the great dead whose words it was his duty to teach.

The Jeep came up unprotestingly from the fluffy snow. It looked happy to be penned in the garage with Elaine's station wagon, and the skis, and the oiled band saw, and the power mower tensely waiting for spring. Ethan was happy, precariously so, so that rather than break he uttered a sound: 'Becky?'

'Yeah?'

'You want to know what else Mr Langley said?'

'What?' They trudged towards the porch, up the path the gentle rake had cleared.

'He said you ski better than the boys.'

'I bet,' she said, and raced to the porch, and in the precipitate way, evasive and female and pleased, that she flung herself to the top step he glimpsed something generic and joyous, a pageant that would leave him behind.

Sylvia Plath

The Fifteen Dollar Eagle

There are other tattoo shops in Madigan Square, but none of them a patch on Carmey's place. He's a real poet with the needle and dye, an artist with a heart. Kids, dock bums, the out-of-town couples in for a beer put on the brakes in front of Carmey's, nose-to-the-window, one and all. You got a dream, Carmey says, without saying a word, you got a rose on the heart, an eagle in the muscle, you got the sweet Jesus himself, so come in to me. Wear your heart on your skin in this life, I'm the man can give you a deal. Dogs, wolves, horses and lions for the animal lover. For the ladies, butterflies, birds of paradise, baby heads smiling or in tears, take your choice. Roses, all sorts, large, small, bud and full bloom, roses with name scrolls, roses with thorns, roses with Dresden-doll heads sticking up in dead centre, pink petal, green leaf, set off smart by a lead-black line. Snakes and dragons for Frankenstein. Not to mention cow-girls, hula girls, mermaids and movie queens, ruby-nippled and bare as you please. If you've got a back to spare, there's Christ on the cross, a thief at either elbow and angels overhead to right and left holding up a scroll with 'Mount Calvary' on it in Old English script, close as yellow can get to gold.

Outside they point at the multi-coloured pictures plastered on Carmey's three walls, ceiling to floor. They mutter like a mob scene, you can hear them through the glass:

'Honey, take a looka those peacocks!'

'That's crazy, paying for tattoos. I only paid for one I got, a panther on my arm.'

'You want a heart, I'll tell him where.'

I see Carmey in action for the first time courtesy of my steady man, Ned Bean. Lounging against a wall of hearts and flowers, waiting for business, Carmey is passing the time of day with a Mr Tomolillo, an extremely small person wearing a wool jacket that drapes his non-existent shoulders without any attempt at fit or reformation. The jacket is patterned with brown squares the size of cigarette packs, each square boldly outlined in black. You could play tick-tack-toe on it. A brown fedora hugs his head just above the eyebrows like the cap on a mushroom. He has the thin, rapt, triangular face of a praying mantis. As Ned introduces me, Mr Tomolillo snaps over from the waist in a bow neat as the little moustache hairlining his upper lip. I can't help admiring this bow because the shop is so crowded there's barely room for the four of us to stand up without bumping elbows and knees at the slightest move.

The whole place smells of gunpowder and some fumey antiseptic. Ranged along the back wall from left to right are: Carmey's work table, electric needles hooked to a rack over a Lazy Susan of dye pots, Carmey's swivel chair facing the show window, a straight customer's chair facing Carmey's chair, a waste bucket, and an orange crate covered with scraps of paper and pencil stubs. At the front of the shop, next to the glass door, there is another straight chair, with the big placard of Mount Calvary propped on it, and a cardboard file-drawer on a scuffed wooden table. Among the babies and daisies on the wall over Carmey's chair hang two faded sepia daguerreotypes of a boy from the waist up, one front-view, one back, from the distance he seems to be wearing a long-sleeved, skin-tight black lace shirt. A closer look shows he is stark naked, covered only with a creeping ivy of tattoos.

In a jaundiced clipping from some long-ago rotogravure, these Oriental men and women are sitting crosslegged on tasselled cushions, back to the camera and embroidered with seven-headed dragons, mountain ranges, cherry trees and waterfalls. 'These people have not a stitch of clothing on,' the blurb points out. 'They belong to a society in which tattoos are required for membership. Sometimes a full job costs as much as $300.' Next to this, a photograph of a bald man's head with the tentacles of an octopus just rounding the top of the scalp from the rear.

'Those skins are valuable as many a painting, I imagine,' says Mr Tomolillo. 'If you had them stretched on a board.'

But the Tattooed Boy and those clubby Orientals have nothing on Carmey, who is himself a living advertisement of his art – a schooner in full sail over a rose-and-holly-leaf ocean on his right biceps, Gypsy Rose Lee flexing her muscled belly on the left, forearms jammed with hearts, stars and anchors, lucky numbers and name scrolls, indigo edges blurred so he reads like a comic strip left out in a Sunday rainstorm. A fan of the Wild West, Carmey is rumoured to have a bronco reared from navel to collar-bone, a thistle-stubborn cowboy stuck to its back. But that may be a mere fable inspired by his habit of wearing tooled leather cowboy boots, finely heeled, and a Bill Hickock belt studded with red stones to hold up his black chino slacks. Carmey's eyes are blue. A blue in no way inferior to the much sung about skies of Texas.

'I been at it sixteen years now,' Carmey says, leaning back against his picture-book wall, 'and you might say I'm still learning. My first job was in Maine, during the war. They heard I was a tattooist and called me out to this station of W.A.C.s.'

'To tat*too* them?' I ask.

'To tattoo their numbers on, nothing more or less.'

'Weren't some of them scared?'

'Oh, sure, sure. But some of them came back. I got two Wacs in one day for a tattoo. Well they hemmed. And they hawed. "Look," I tell them, "you came in the other day and you knew which one you wanted, what's the trouble?"

' "Well it's not what we want but where we want it," one of them pipes up. "Well if that's all it is you can trust me," I say. "I'm like a doctor, see? I handle so many women it means nothing." "Well I want three roses," this one says: "one on my stomach and one on each cheek of my butt." So the other one gets up courage, you know how it is, and asks for one rose . . .'

'Little ones or big ones?' Mr Tomolillo won't let a detail slip.

'About like that up there,' Carmey points to a card of roses on the wall, each bloom the size of a Brussels sprout. 'The biggest going. So I did the roses and told them: "Ten dollars off the price if you come back and show them to me when the scab's gone." '

'Did they come?' Ned wants to know.

'You bet they did.' Carmey blows a smoke ring that hangs wavering in the air a foot from his nose, the blue, vaporous outline of a cabbage-rose.

'You wanta know,' he says, 'a crazy law? I could tattoo you anywhere,' he looks me over with great care, 'anywhere at all. Your back. Your rear.' His eyelids droop, you'd think he was praying. 'Your breasts. Anywhere at all but your face, hands and feet.'

Mr Tomolillo asks: 'Is that a *Federal* law?'

Carmey nodds. 'A Federal law. I got a blind,' he juts a thumb at the dusty-slatted venetian blind drawn up in the display window. 'I let that blind down, and I can do privately any part of the body. Except face, hands and feet.'

'I bet it's because they *show*,' I say.

'Sure. Take the Army, at drill. The guys wouldn't look right. Their faces and hands would stand out, they couldn't cover up.'

'However that may be,' Mr Tomolillo says, 'I think it is a shocking law, a totalitarian law. There should be a freedom about personal adornment in any democracy. I mean, if a lady *wants* a rose on the back of her hand, I should think . . .'

'She should *have* it,' Carmey finishes with heat. 'People

should have what they want, regardless. Why, I had a little lady in here the other day,' Carmey levels the air with the flat of his hand not five feet from the floor. 'So high. Wanted Calvary, the whole works, on her back, and I gave it to her. Eighteen hours it took.'

I eyed the thieves and angels on the poster of Mount Calvary with some doubt. 'Didn't you have to shrink it down a bit?'

'Nope.'

'Or leave off an angel?' Ned wonders. 'Or a bit of the foreground?'

'Not a bit of it. A thirty-five dollar job in full colour, thieves, angels, Old English – the works. She went out of the shop proud as punch. It's not every little lady's got all Calvary in full colour on her back. Oh, I copy photos people bring in, I copy movie stars. Anything they want, I do it. I've got some designs I wouldn't put up on the wall on account of offending some of the clients. I'll show you.' Carmey opens the cardboard file drawer on the table at the front of the shop. 'The wife's got to clean this up,' he says. 'It's a terrible mess.'

'Does your wife help you?' I ask with interest.

'Oh, Laura, she's in the shop most of the day.' For some reason Carmey sounds all at once solemn as a monk on Sunday. I wonder, does he use her for a come-on: Laura, the Tattooed Lady, a living masterpiece, sixteen years in the making. Not a white patch on her, ladies and gentlemen – look all you want to. 'You should drop by and keep her company, she likes talk.' He is rummaging around in the drawer, not coming up with anything, when he stops in his tracks and stiffens like a pointer.

This big guy is standing in the doorway.

'What can I do for you?' Carmey steps forward, the maestro he is.

'I want that eagle you showed me.'

Ned and Mr Tomolillo and I flatten ourselves against the side walls to let the guy into the middle of the room. He'll be a sailor out of uniform in his pea jacket and plaid wool shirt. His diamond-shaped head, width all between the ears, tapers up to a narrow plateau of cropped black hair.

'The nine dollar or the fifteen?'

'The fifteen.'

Mr Tomolillo sighs in gentle admiration.

The sailor sits down in the chair facing Carmey's swivel, shrugs out of his peajacket, unbuttons his left shirt cuff and begins slowly to roll up the sleeve.

'You come right in here,' Carmey says to me in a low, promising voice, 'where you can get a good look. You've never seen a tattooing before.' I squinch up and settle on the crate of papers in the corner at the left of Carmey's chair, careful as a hen on eggs.

Carmey flicks through the cardboard file again and this time digs out a square piece of plastic. 'Is this the one?'

The sailor looks at the eagle pricked out on the plastic. Then he says: 'That's right,' and hands it back to Carmey.

'Mmmm,' Mr Tomolillo murmurs in honour of the sailor's taste.

Ned says, 'That's a fine eagle."

The sailor straightens with a certain pride. Carmey is dancing round him now, laying a dark-stained burlap cloth across his lap, arranging a sponge, a razor, various jars with smudged-out labels and a bowl of antiseptic on his work-table – finicky as a priest whetting his machete for the fatted calf. Everything has to be just so. Finally he sits down. The sailor holds out his left arm as Ned and Mr Tomolillo close in behind his chair, Ned leaning over the sailor's right shoulder and Mr Tomolillo over his left. At Carmey's elbow I have the best view of all.

With a close, quick swipe of the razor, Carmey clears the sailor's forearm of its black springing hair, wiping the hair off the blade's edge and on to the floor with his thumb. Then he anoints the area of bared flesh with vaseline from a small jar on top of his table, 'You ever been tattooed before?'

'Yeah.' The sailor is no gossip. 'Once.' Already his eyes are locked in a vision of something on the far side of Carmey's head, through the walls and away in the thin air beyond the four of us in the room.

Carmey is sprinkling a black powder on the face of the plastic square and rubbing the powder into the pricked holes. The outline of the eagle darkens. With one flip, Carmey presses the plastic square powder-side against the sailor's greased arm. When he peels the plastic off, easy as skin off an onion, the outline of an eagle, wings spread, claws hooked for action, frowns up from the sailor's arm.

'Ah!' Mr Tomolillo rocks back on his cork heels and casts a meaning look at Ned. Ned raises his eyebrows in approval. The sailor allows himself a little quirk of the lip. On him it is as good as a smile.

'Now,' Carmey takes down one of the electric needles, pitching it rabbit-out-of-the-hat, 'I am going to show you how we make a nine dollar eagle a fifteen dollar eagle.'

He presses a button on the needle. Nothing happens.

'Well,' he sighs, 'it's not working.'

Mr Tomolillo groans. 'Not again?'

Then something strikes Carmey and he laughs and flips a switch on the wall behind him. This time when he presses the needle it buzzes and sparks blue. 'No connexion, that's what it was.'

'Thank heaven,' says Mr Tomolillo.

Carmey fills the needle from a pot of black dye on the Lazy Susan. 'This same eagle,' Carmey lowers the needle to the eagle's right wingtip, 'for nine dollars is only black and red. For the fifteen dollars you're going to see a blend of four colours.' The needle steers along the lines laid by the powder. 'Black, green, brown and red. We're out of blue at the moment or it'd be five colours.' The needle skips and back-talks like a pneumatic drill but Carmey's hand is steady as a surgeon's. 'How I *love* eagles!'

'I believe you *live* on Uncle Sam's eagles,' says Mr Tomolillo.

Black ink seeps over the curve of the sailor's arm and into

the stiff, stained butcher's apron canvas covering his lap, but the needle travels on, scalloping the wing feathers from tip to root. Bright beads of red are rising through the ink, heart's blood bubbles smearing out into the black stream.

'The guys complain,' Carmey singsongs. 'Week after week I get the same complaining: What have you got new? We don't want the same type eagle, red and black. So I figure out this blend. You wait. A solid colour eagle.'

The eagle is losing itself in a spreading thundercloud of black ink. Carmey stops, sloshes his needle in the bowl of antiseptic, and a geyser of white blooms up to the surface from the bowl's bottom. Then Carmey dips a big, round cinnamon-coloured sponge in the bowl and wipes away the ink from the sailor's arm. The eagle emerges from its hood of bloodied ink, a raised outline on the raw skin.

'Now you're gonna see something.' Carmey twirls the Lazy Susan till the pot of green is under his thumb and picks another needle from the rack.

The sailor is gone from behind his eyes now, off somewhere in Tibet, Uganda or the Barbados, oceans and continents away from the blood drops jumping in the wake of the wide green swaths Carmey is drawing in the shadow of the eagle's wings.

About this time I notice an odd sensation. A powerful sweet perfume is rising from the sailor's arm. My eyes swerve from the mingling red and green and I find myself staring intently into the waste bucket by my left side. As I watch the calm rubble of coloured candy wrappers, cigarette butts and old wads of muddily-stained Kleenex, Carmey tosses a tissue soaked with fresh red on to the heap. Behind the silhouetted heads of Ned and Mr Tomolillo the panthers, roses and red-nippled ladies wink and jitter. If I fall forward or to the right, I will jog Carmey's elbow and make him stab the sailor and ruin a perfectly good fifteen-dollar eagle not to mention disgracing my sex. The only alternative is a dive into the bucket of bloody papers.

'I'm doing the brown now,' Carmey sings out a mile away,

and my eyes rivet again on the sailor's blood-sheened arm. 'When the eagle heals, the colours will blend right into each other, like on a painting.'

Ned's face is a scribble of black India ink on a seven-colour crazy-quilt.

'I'm going . . .' I make my lips move, but no sound comes out.

Ned starts towards me but before he gets there the room switches off like a light.

The next thing is, I am looking into Carmey's shop from a cloud with the X-ray eyes of an angel and hearing the tiny sound of a bee spitting blue fire.

'The blood got her?' It is Carmey's voice, small and far.

'She looks all white,' says Mr Tomolillo. 'And her eyes are funny.'

Carmey passes something to Mr Tomolillo. 'Have her sniff that.' Mr Tomolillo hands something to Ned. 'But not too much.'

Ned holds something to my nose.

I sniff, and I am sitting in the chair at the front of the shop with Mount Calvary as a back-rest. I sniff again. Nobody looks angry so I have not bumped Carmey's needle. Ned is screwing the cap on a little flask of yellow liquid. Yardley's smelling salts.

'Ready to go back?' Mr Tomolillo points kindly to the deserted orange crate.

'Almost.' I have a strong instinct to stall for time. I whisper in Mr Tomolillo's ear which is very near to me, he is so short, 'Do *you* have any tattoos?'

Under the mushroom-brim of his fedora Mr Tomolillo's eyes roll heavenward. 'My gracious no! I'm only here to see about the springs. The springs in Mr Carmichael's machine have a way of breaking in the middle of a customer.'

'How annoying.'

'That's what I'm here for. We're testing out a new spring now, a much heavier spring. You know how distressing it is when you're in the dentist's chair and your mouth is full of what-not . . .'

'Balls of cotton and little metal siphons . . .?'

'Precisely. And in the middle of this the dentist turns away,' Mr Tomolillo half-turns his back in illustration and makes an evil, secretive face, 'and buzzes about in the corner for ten minutes with the machinery, you don't know what.' Mr Tomolillo's face smooths out like linen under a steam iron. 'That's what I'm here to see about, a stronger spring. A spring that won't let a customer down.'

By this time I am ready to go back to my seat of honour on the orange crate. Carmey has just finished with the brown and in my absence the inks have indeed blended into one another. Against the shaven skin, the lacerated eagle is swollen in tri-coloured fury, claws curved sharp as butcher's hooks.

'I think we could redden the eye a little?'

The sailor nods, and Carmey opens the lid on a pot of dye the colour of tomato ketchup. As soon as he stops working with the needle, the sailor's skin sends up its blood beads, not just from the bird's black outline now, but from the whole rasped, rainbowed body.

'Red,' Carmey says, 'really picks things up.'

'Do you save the blood?' Mr Tomolillo asks suddenly.

'I should think,' says Ned, 'you might well have some arrangement with the Red Cross.'

'With a blood bank!' The smelling salts have blown my head clear as a blue day on Monadnock. 'Just put a little basin on the floor to catch the drippings.'

Carmey is picking out a red eye on the eagle. 'We vampires don't share our blood.' The eagle's eye reddens but there is now no telling blood from ink. 'You never heard of a vampire doing that, did you?'

'Nooo . . .' Mr Tomolillo admits.

Carmey floods the flesh behind the eagle with red and the finished eagle poises on a red sky, born and baptized in the blood of its owner.

The sailor drifts back from parts unknown.

'Nice?' With his sponge Carmey clears the eagle of the blood filming its colours the way a sidewalk artist might blow the pastel dust from a drawing of the White House, Liz Taylor or Lassie-Come-Home.

'I always say,' the sailor remarks to nobody in particular, 'when you get a tattoo, get a good one. Nothing but the best.' He looks down at the eagle which has begun in spite of Carmey's swabbing to bleed again. There is a little pause. Carmey is waiting for something and it isn't money. 'How much to write Japan under that?'

Carmey breaks into a pleased smile. 'One dollar.'

'Write Japan, then.'

Carmey marks out the letters on the sailor's arm, an extra flourish to the J's hook, the loop of the P, and the final N, a love-letter to the eagle-conquered Orient. He fills the needle and starts on the J.

'I *understand*,' Mr Tomolillo observes in his clear, lecturer's voice, 'Japan is a centre of tattooing.'

'Not when *I* was there,' the sailor says. 'It's banned.'

'Banned!' says Ned. 'What for?'

'Oh, they think it's *bar*barous nowadays.' Carmey doesn't lift his eyes from the second A, the needle responding like a broken-in bronc under his masterly thumb. 'There are operators, of course. *Sub rosa*. There always are.' He puts the final curl on the N and sponges off the wellings of blood which seem bent on obscuring his artful lines. 'That what you wanted?'

'That's it.'

Carmey folds a wad of Kleenex into a rough bandage and lays it over the eagle and Japan. Spry as a shopgirl wrapping a gift package he tapes the tissue into place.

The sailor gets up and hitches into his peajacket. Several schoolboys, lanky, with pale, pimply faces, are crowding the doorway, watching. Without a word the sailor takes out his wallet and peels sixteen dollar bills off a green roll. Carmey transfers the cash to his wallet. The schoolboys fall back to let the sailor pass into the street.

'I hope you didn't mind my getting dizzy.'

Carmey grins. 'Why do you think I've got those salts so close to hand? I have big guys passing out cold. They get egged in here by their buddie and don't know how to get out of it. I got people getting sick to their ears in that bucket.'

'She's never got like that before,' Ned says. 'She's seen all sorts of blood. Babies born. Bull fights. Things like that.'

'You was all worked up.' Carmey offers me a cigarette, which I accept, takes one himself, and Ned takes one, and Mr Tomolillo says no thank you. 'You was all tensed, that's what did it.'

'How much is a heart?'

The voice comes from a kid in a black leather jacket in the front of the shop. His buddies nudge each other and let out harsh, puppy-barks of laughter. The boy grins and flushes all at once under his purple stipple of acne. 'A heart with a scroll under it and a name on the scroll.'

Carmey leans back in his swivel chair and digs his thumbs into his belt. The cigarette wobbles on his bottom lip. 'Four dollars,' he says without batting an eye.

'Four dollars?' The boy's voice swerves up and cracks in shrill disbelief. The three of them in the doorway mutter among themselves and shuffle back and forth.

'Nothing here in the heart line under three dollars.' Carmey doesn't kowtow to the tight-fisted. You want a rose, you want a heart in this life, you pay for it. Through the nose.

The boy wavers in front of the placard of hearts on the wall, pink, lush hearts, hearts with arrows through them, hearts in the centre of buttercup wreaths. 'How much,' he asks in a small, craven voice, 'for just a name?'

'One dollar.' Carmey's tone is strictly business.

The boy holds out his left hand. 'I want Ruth.' He draws an imaginary line across his left wrist. 'Right here . . . so I can cover it up with a watch if I want to.'

His two friends guffaw from the doorway.

Carmey points to the straight chair and lays his half-smoked cigarette on the Lazy Susan between two dye-pots. The boy sits down, schoolbooks balanced on his lap.

'What happens,' Mr Tomolillo asks of the world in general, 'if you choose to change a name? Do you just cross if off and write the next above it?'

'You could,' Ned suggests, 'wear a watch over the old name so only the new name showed.'

'And then another watch,' I say, 'over that, when there's a third name.'

'Until your arm,' Mr Tomolillo nods, 'is up to the shoulder with watches.'

Carmey is shaving the thin scraggly growth of hairs from the boy's wrist. 'You're taking a lot of ragging from somebody.'

The boy stares at his wrist with a self-conscious and unsteady smile, a smile that is maybe only a public substitute for tears. With his right hand he clutches his schoolbooks to keep them from sliding off his knee.

Carmey finishes marking R-U-T-H on the boy's wrist and holds the needle poised. 'She'll bawl you out when she sees this.' But the boy nods him to go ahead.

'Why?' Ned asks. 'Why should she bawl him out?'

'Gone and got yourself tattooed!' Carmey mimics a mincing disgust. 'And with just a name! Is *that* all you think of me? – She'll be wanting roses, birds, butterflies . . .' The needle sticks for a second and the boy flinches like a colt. 'And if you *do* get all that stuff to please her – roses . . .'

'Birds and butterflies,' Mr Tomolillo puts in.

' . . . she'll say, sure as rain at a ball game: What'd you want to go and spend all that *money* for?' Carmey whizzes the needle clean in the bowl of antiseptic. 'You can't beat a woman.' A few meagre blood drops stand up along the four letters – letters so black and plain you can hardly tell it's a tattoo and not just inked in with a pen. Carmey tapes a narrow bandage of Kleenex over the name. The whole operation lasts less than ten minutes.

The boy fishes a crumpled dollar bill from his back pocket. His friends cuff him fondly on the shoulder and the three of them crowd out of the door, all at the same time, nudging, pushing, tripping over their feet. Several faces, limpet-pale against the window, melt away as Carmey's eye lingers on them.

'No wonder he doesn't want a heart, that kid, he wouldn't know what to do with it. He'll be back next week asking for a Betty or a Dolly or some such, you wait.' He sighs, and goes to the cardboard file and pulls out a stack of those photographs he wouldn't put on the wall and passes them around. 'One picture I would like to get,' Carmey leans back in the swivel chair and props his cowboy boots on a little carton. 'The butterfly. I got pictures of the rabbit hunt. I got pictures of ladies with snakes winding up their legs and into them, but I could make a lot of sweet dough if I got a picture of the butterfly on a woman.'

'Some queer kind of butterfly nobody wants?' Ned peers in the general direction of my stomach as at some high-grade saleable parchment.

'It's not what, it's where. One wing on the front of each thigh. You know how butterflies on a flower make their wings flutter, ever so little? Well, any move a woman makes, these wings look to be going in and out, in and out. I'd like a photograph of that so much I'd practically do a butterfly for free.'

I toy, for a second, with the thought of a New Guinea Golden, wings extending from hip-bone to knee-cap, ten times life-size, but drop it fast. A fine thing if I got tired of my own skin sooner than last year's sack.

'Plenty of women *ask* for butterflies in that particular spot,' Carmey goes on, 'but you know what, not one of them will let a photograph be taken after the job's done. Not even from the waist down. Don't imagine I haven't asked. You'd think everybody over the whole United States would recognize them from the way they carry on when it's even mentioned.'

'Couldn't,' Mr Tomolillo ventures shyly, 'the wife oblige? Make it a little family affair?'

Carmey's face screws up in a pained way. 'Naw,' he shakes his head, his voice weighted with an old wonder and regret. 'Naw, Laura won't hear of the needle. I used to think the idea of it'd grow on her after a bit, but nothing doing. She makes me feel, sometimes, what do I see in it all. Laura's white as the day she was born. Why, she *hates* tattoos.'

Up to this moment I have been projecting, fatuously, intimate visits with Laura at Carmey's place. I have been imagining a lithe, supple Laura, a butterfly poised for flight on each breast, roses blooming on her buttocks, a gold guarding dragon on her back and Sinbad the Sailor in six colours on her belly, a woman with Experience written all over her, a woman to learn from in this life. I should have known better.

The four of us are slumped there in a smog of cigarette smoke, not saying a word, when a round, muscular woman comes into the shop, followed closely by a greasy-haired man with a dark, challenging expression. The woman is wrapped to the chin in a woolly electric-blue coat; a fuchsia kerchief covers all but the pompadour of her glinting blonde hair. She sits down in the chair in front of the window regardless of Mount Calvary and proceeds to stare fixedly at Carmey. The man stations himself next to her and keeps a severe eye on Carmey too, as if expecting him to bolt without warning.

There is a moment of potent silence.

'Why,' Carmey says pleasantly, but with small heart, 'here's the wife now.'

I take a second look at the woman and rise from my comfortable seat on the crate at Carmey's elbow. Judging from his watchdog stance, I gather the strange man is either Laura's brother or her bodyguard or a low-class private detective in her employ. Mr Tomolillo and Ned are moving with one accord towards the door.

'We must be running along,' I murmur, since nobody else seems inclined to speak.

'Say hello to the people, Laura,' Carmey begs, back to the wall. I can't help but feel sorry for him, even a little ashamed. The starch is gone out of Carmey now, and the gay talk.

Laura doesn't say a word. She is waiting with the large calm of a cow for the three of us to clear out. I imagine her body, death-lily-white and totally bare – the body of a woman immune as a nun to the eagle's anger, the desire of the rose. From Carmey's wall the world's menagerie howls and ogles at her alone.

Emanuel Litvinoff

The Geography Lesson

We were standing under the shelter during break, shivering in our jerseys. A water-logged morning, rain scudding under a nasty gale and the sky – what you could see of it – wrinkled and sodden like a sheet dipped in the wash. It was better to be jailed in class and we waited morosely for the bell.

Shmulevitch searched in his pockets and produced a grubby acid drop. 'On'y got one,' he mumbled, slipping it quickly into his mouth. He sucked noisily and wiped his nose with his sleeve: he disgusted me. I wandered hopefully over to a group of boys round Morry Schein who bought sweets by the pound when he was flush.

'Oy, Morry-boy!' I called, though I didn't like him all that much. His family kept a barber-shop in Bethnal Green Road and he put on brilliantine. It only made him smell worse.

But Morry took no notice. He was in a state of excitement and so were the others. 'Yer telling a lie!' a boy said, running his tongue over his lips. 'Din' I tell ya I seen it?' Scheiny insisted, mouth dribbling. I drew closer, fascinated. 'Let's ask Litty,' someone suggested. ' 'E's a rill bookworm.'

'You fink they write about it in books?' Morry Schein said scornfully. 'No good asking old Four-Eyes. Never seen a tit, even!'

'What's the argument?' I inquired loftily, taking off my glasses.

'It's Morry's shiksa,' Siddy Kravitz said. 'She let's 'im see 'er with no close. Starkers!'

'What about his shiksa, then?'

'Morry says the knish is at the back, by the toochus. She sits on it.'

'Bollocks!' one of the boys exploded. 'I bet my sister don't!'

'Maybe shiksas is different,' Siddy argued. What d'you say, Lit?' He sat next to me in class and copied my sums, so my judgement was respected.

'Religion's got nothing to do with it,' I announced flatly. 'Everybody's got it in the same place, boys and girls. It's biology.'

Morry was enraged. 'I seen it, you didn't!' he shouted. 'Betcha hundred pounds I'm right! Betcha million!'

Shmulevitch ambled up and joined the argument. 'Joo know where the knish is?' Scheiny asked him. Shmuly looked puzzled. 'On a gel, you dope!' Scheiny yelled.

'Dahn 'ere,' said Shmuly. He touched himself between the legs.

'I'll prove it!' Morry threatened darkly. 'I'll letcha see.' We crowded round. 'When?' ''Ow can yer?' 'Don't berlieve!'

'Orlright, we'll see after school. I'll tell 'er to take off 'er bloomers an' bend dahn near the key'ole.'

When break was over, Parker, our master, distributed books and atlases for the geography lesson. He talked in a bored voice about Africa, surreptitiously picking his hairy nostrils. Outside the window, factory chimneys swirled in clouds of grit and trains trundling towards Liverpool Street Station vibrated the floor of the classroom. My forefinger traced the profile of Africa, lions prowling the forests of my brain. Suddenly Parker strode on spindly legs between the desks and thwacked his stick across my back. Siddy Kravitz, beside me, winced. 'I've got eyes at the back of my head!' Parker snarled into my startled face, but he returned to the front of the class in good humour and told us we could read the geography books to ourselves as long as we ignore the pictures of naked black ladies. Baring his long teeth in a sinister smile, he went off for a smoke.

Morry Schein passed me a note. There was a drawing of

something that looked like a vertical eye with a line down the length of it. Underneath was written: 'YOU.' I screwed it up, soaked it in the inkwell and chucked it at him. It hit the boy behind him on the head. He chucked it back and soon everybody was at it. Parker arrived while it was going on and enthusiastically caned six of us, including me.

Going home for dinner, I thought about Morry and the shiksa. The Scheins were rich and she was their servant, but I couldn't believe she'd let him actually *see* her without bloomers. He might have spied on her when she washed, or drilled a hole in the lavatory, but nobody had a knish where he said she did! I fingered myself and tried to imagine I was a girl, but it still seemed improbable. We'd just got a girl in our family a few weeks before and I'd watched my mother change its napkin, but all I ever saw was a kind of crease between its bandy legs.

It was a long day at school, and when it was over Morry Schein tried to sneak away. He'd always been a big mouth. We chased after him – Siddy Kravitz, Shmulevitch and me. 'Y'promised!' Siddy said indignantly.

'I changed my mind,' Morry said, breaking into a run. Shmuly caught him and put Chinese torture on his wrist, so he changed his mind again and said he'd do it after tea. But only for a minute. 'You better not be late,' he said. 'I gotta go ter Hebrew or my dad'll murder me.'

The three of us met by arrangement. Shmulevitch had to bring his brother along in the pram because their mother served on a fish-stall during the evening busy. I was shivering inside and my face felt on fire despite the cold.

'I'm only going 'cause Morry dared me,' I said.

Siddy Kravitz looked miserable and excited. 'Yer,' he said. 'Me, too.'

It was raining hard as we trudged up to Bethnal Green Road, getting splashed with mud as we steered Shmuly's pram into the gaps between lorries and buses to Schein's Gentleman's Hairdressing Saloon. It was quiet there at that time of the day. A man in a butcher's apron read a Yiddish newspaper, waiting while old Schein scraped soap off a fat man's chin, poured Levy's Patent Hair Restorer from a coloured bottle over the thin strands of ruffled hair on his pink scalp and gave him a friction.

Morry came to the door of the side entrance, looking shifty. 'You wanna play with my Meccano?' he asked in a low voice.

'No!' Shmuly hissed. 'We wanna see what yer said. The shiksa.'

The shop cat crept up stealthily and rubbed its back against Morry's leg. He picked it up and stroked the black fur. 'Look,' he said, 'this proves it,' and, lifting the animal's tail, pointed hopefully at the slit in its bottom.

'We didn't come 'ere in the bleaten rain just to see a cat's shitty arse!' Shmulevitch protested. 'I could a stayed 'ome an' done that!'

'Well, I don' know if she's in 'er room.'

Siddy Kravitz gave Morry a push. 'Gorn, let's go up, then.'

We parked the pram in the passage and followed Morry up the stairs, tiptoeing and giggling.

'Don' make so much soddin' noise!' Morry whispered frantically. 'It's right up in the attic.' When we reached it, he hesitated, then knocked timidly on the door. 'Jinny, are you in?' he called. 'Jinny, it's me, Morry.'

'Piss off!' someone said distinctly, a female. 'I'm busy.'

After some argument, the door was opened and he was admitted. We crept out of hiding and jostled to reach the keyhole. Siddy Kravitz got there first. He knelt on one knee and placed his eye against the aperture. 'C'n y'see?' Shmuly asked. Siddy shushed him.

Morry's voice came to us through the door. 'Do whatcha done last time, Jinny,' he coaxed.

We heard Jinny laugh. 'Dunno whatcha talkin' abaht.'

'Y'do know.'

'It's wicked. I'll tell yer dad.'

Shmuly began to get very excited. 'Its my turn,' he insisted and after a brief scuffle replaced Kravitz at the keyhole. 'I kin see a bed,' he reported eagerly. 'Could see more if Morry wasn't in the way.'

The girl inside was laughing again. I got down and scraped my knees on the bare wooden floor but managed to get a peep into the room when Shmulevitch shifted. An unmade bed stood against the faded, flowered-patterned wall and a skinny girl of about sixteen came into the line of sight. She sat on the edge of the bed and smiled wickedly.

'Who's yer darling, then?' she teased.

We heard Morry groan.

'Won't do it, then. Y'gotta say it nice. Who's yer darling?'

'Aw, right!' said Morry. 'You are.'

'I'm what?'

I began to feel an irresistible tickle in my chest. There was some confused movement inside and I suddenly saw some flesh close-up. 'She's done it!' I was awed and slightly scared.

Shmuly pushed me aside to see for himself. He gazed intensely for a moment, then said in outraged disappointment: 'It's Morry's knee!' When I laughed, he punched me. But he began to laugh himself and, after trying to stop us, Siddy found he couldn't stop laughing, either.

Morry's shiksa suddenly pulled open the door and she wasn't undressed at all. We scampered hastily down the stairs, making a terrible noise, grabbed Shmuly's pram and ran yelling into the rain. Old man Schein came out of the shop with a razor in his hand shouting Yiddish curses. We didn't stop running until we got among the evening crowds in Brick Lane market. Rain sizzled on the naptha flares and gusts of wind flapped the tarpaulin covering of stalls. We didn't feel like laughing any more.

'Never saw nothin'! Did we?' Siddy Kravitz said dejectedly. He stared defiantly at us. 'I'd a called 'er darling. Just to know.'

Shmulevitch, looking preoccupied, steered his pram close

to the edge of the pavement. When he rejoined us, he lifted up the waterproof apron to show some apples lying by the fat legs of his little brother. 'Nicked 'em,' he said with huge satisfaction.

The kid woke up and began to cry.

Emanuel Litvinoff

The Battle for Mendel Shaffer

Mendel Shaffer lived in a flat on the third floor of our building with his grandmother and Mr Schulberg, the lodger, a small fat man of anxious countenance who was a collector for the Jewish Burial Society. His father, like mine, was away in Russia at the time and his mother had run off to America with a Lithuanian tailor so long before that the episode was little more than a scandalous legend in my day. Because of this there was hardly a Jewish mother in the street who did not melt with compassion at poor Mendel's plight or try to force some delicacy upon him when he passed with the shy and stricken look of one who would rather go unnoticed.

He was a quiet, studious boy of precocious gravity that came of living in the company of elderly folk. His grandmother, a devout woman, wanted him to be a rabbinical scholar, a musician, or a doctor. Nobody thought her foolish in these lofty ambitions, for Mendel was both clever and talented. An old head on young shoulders, the neighbours commented approvingly, and oh! how he played the fiddle! like an angel – entirely self-taught. They would get him to perform at celebrations, drawing Yiddish melodies from the strings in a piercing, uncertain tone that made them snuffle into their handkerchiefs.

The story of that fiddle was one of our folk legends. His grandmother got it from the rag-and-bone man in exchange for a leaking copper samovar. She took it home, polished it carefully, then held it out. 'Play, Mendel,' she said simply. Mendel had been playing ever since.

But what he did most was read, preferably encyclopedias. He liked to surprise us with stupendous facts. It was Mendel who first told me that King Solomon had seven hundred wives and three hundred concubines, that the female mantis consumes its mate in nuptial frenzy, that the Chinese alphabet boasts more than 40,000 characters, and other things that have stuck in my mind like burrs. He tried to learn a few stupendous facts like that every day, partly, I think, because ordinary conversation did not come easily to him and it helped to have something spectacular to talk about.

Mendel Shaffer's grandmother made buttonholes for a living. She worked at home on the bedroom table while Mendel read, practised the violin or lay at night dreaming eruditely under the hissing gaslight. Two evenings a week Susskind, the Hebrew teacher, left the cellar in Kerbela Street where he lived and gave the boy private tuition in the holy books. Afterwards, he drank a glass of lemon tea with Mr Schulberg and the grandmother, calling his pupil 'The little rabbi' and praising his precocity. The old woman listened shrewdly, counting the flatteries like the coins in her purse, while Schulberg noisily sucked his tea and confirmed the praise with ingratiating nods and eager grimaces.

There were other clever and talented boys in our neighbourhood, some of them now men of wealth and fame, but I cannot recall anyone who was nurtured so strictly as Mendel. His wasn't really much of a life for a boy of ten. When the rest of us were kicking a ball in the street, or wandering among the fruit stalls of the market-place as rapacious as hungry foxes, Mendel was unable to move a hundred yards without being trapped by his grandmother's jealous vigilance. It was his soul she guarded as much as his safety. She kept him unnaturally clean in the eyes of God, both in person and in conduct, as if he were the son of the Chief Rabbi himself.

One stifling afternoon during some Jewish festival or other, when the brick streets of the East End gave off a more than usual stench of overcrowding and decay, I wandered around, bored and restless, looking for someone to accompany me to Victoria Park. After several rejections, I came to Mendel. I spoke persuasively of grass, trees, the cool water of the lake, my throat dry with grit and desperation. Eventually, he agreed to ask permission to accompany me. But when I went to call him, he was squatting disconsolately on the floor at home, his ankle tethered to the leg of a table by a ridiculously flimsy piece of string. Mr Schulberg, sweating with anxiety, tiptoed from the kitchen and hurried to the door, obviously fleeing from a domestic crisis. Just before he left, he waggled an admonitory forefinger in my face.

I sniggered with embarrassment, Mendel's lower lip trembled and he stared at me like an enemy. After a moment's agonized indecision, he untied himself and stood up just as the old woman entered the room, awesome in her black old-fashioned Sabbath finery. She trailed an atmosphere of claustrophobia and a smell of camphor balls. Her glance was like the wrath of Jehovah and I longed to escape from the cramped piety of the room into the pagan sunshine.

'Sit!' she ordered us harshly, pointing to an ancient horsehair sofa that gave off an odour like the rotted covers of old prayer books. We sat in guilty collusion, avoiding her eyes as she lectured us in a worn, plaintive voice of the need to be steadfast in our faith, to be good Jewish children and to remember how hard it was to bring up fatherless boys in a hostile world. Mendel scraped the scuffed lino with the toe of his boot resentfully. She took his face between her palms and said: 'Don't punish me, Mendel. How long have I got to live?' He began to cry. At the time I thought he was upset by the mention of her death but now I believe it was the roughness of her hands that made him cry, reminding him of how she toiled to support them.

As I left she was crooning endearments, calling him her *feigele*, her little bird.

It was round about that summer that Mendel's father came home, a tall sick-looking man with a big nose jutting from his wasted face like a horny beak. All the children of the tenements were out, shrieking and jeering in their play, as he came limping along the street, a ragged figure with a military pack strapped on his shoulders who trudged past gossiping women and bawling infants with that glazed, exhausted indifference that is seen in soldiers after a long retreat. There was a feverish look in his eyes and we grew uneasy when he stopped and began to scrutinize us, his glance moving uncertainly from one to another. Then he saw Mendel, who was leaning against a window-ledge of the building absorbed in a book. The adam's apple in his skinny neck jumped spasmodically. He took the startled boy in his arms, kissing him over and over again with strange groaning sounds of joy. We all watched shamelessly. A woman sitting on a kitchen chair at her front door covered her face with her apron and wept. Bewildered by the unexpected embrace, Mendel freed himself and gazed mistrustfully at the stranger. Then the two of them stepped out of the sunshine and went together into the gloom of the building.

Mr Shaffer celebrated his return quietly. He was not, it was soon discovered, a particularly sociable man except with children. Instead of inviting the neighbours in for a party, he mixed a large can of ice-cream and dispensed cornets to all the kids of the neighbourhood, smiling and tousling their hair as they came one by one for their free treat. The strains of Mendel's violin were heard in the apartment evening after evening. For a while, he enjoyed unusual popularity among us with stories of his father's tribulation as a soldier in the Russian Revolution, of how he had eaten rats to avoid starvation, lost two toes on his right foot because of frost-bite and spent years in Siberian exile for some political unorthodoxy.

But the sensation soon subsided. Mendel's father became

Mr Shaffer, the cabinet-maker, and his drab comings and goings merged into the familiar pattern of the toiling adult world around us. People wondered if Mr Schulberg, of the Burial Society, would be permitted to remain in the cramped apartment, and if Mr Shaffer would consult the marriage-broker and seek out some young widow to espouse; but it was temporarily decided that he should share a bed with Mr Schulberg until the latter could find another cheap and hospitable lodging, an act of kindness, we thought, for few would wish to live constantly in the company of someone so intimately connected with death.

Acquiring a father unexpectedly like that could be either horrible or marvellous for a boy. In Mendel's case it was marvellous. You'd see the two of them walking hand-in-hand through the raucous streets talking to one another as if no one else in the world existed. They went to museums, parks, art-galleries, visited the Tower, climbed the Monument, inspected the Palace Guard, all things that Mr Shaffer must have dreamed of doing with his son during those long years of waste and deprivation in Russia. If the boy was happy, the man was ecstatic. I saw him one Sunday standing in the market-place utterly dazed by the mounds of ripe fruit, barrels of shmalz herring and pungent strings of sausages, gazing at these and the stalls flowing with coloured silks and heaped with new-smelling leather as if the wonder of the world was spread before his feasting eyes. And the way Mendel smiled up at the tall man you'd think he was the father, not the child.

Mendel was changing in all kinds of ways. He was the sort of boy who ran like a girl, flinging his legs out sideways; who couldn't catch a ball, climb a stack of timber or hitch a ride on the tailboard of a lorry. The more he tried to do these things, the clumsier he became, and he got into the habit of sitting around reading when the rest of us played games. Mr Shaffer observed this once or twice, then began to urge Mendel to join in with the others. Because his father was watching, we felt constrained to be more patient of Mendel's awkwardness. This gave him more confidence and, although most of us continued to out-run and out-jostle him, he was soon quite a star in games that required mental agility as well as physical resources.

But in the meantime rumours of dissension in the Shaffers' apartment began to get around. Now that he was earning a living Mr Shaffer stopped the old woman making button-holes, and the way she grumbled you'd think he had taken the very bread from her mouth instead of easing her labours. She was an obstinate, independent creature designed by nature to rule a tribe, and all that resolute energy was expended on a solitary boy. Now even that was being made superfluous. More and more frequently the pacific Mr Schulberg was seen hurrying from the flat in a frenzy of apprehension. The women would stop him on the stairs and, with an elaborate pretence of incuriosity, ask him this, that and the other, but Mr Schulberg pleaded pressing business and made an agitated departure. It was a little while, therefore, before people discovered that the principal source of contention between the father and grandmother was the soul of Mendel Shaffer.

My mother got the first clue from me. One rainy evening, a few of us were sitting in the doorway of the tenement staring at the reflection of street lamps on the wet, twilit pavements. This induced a sort of philosophic melancholy. As Mr Shaffer came by from work and gave us a tired greeting, the talk had got around to God. He was half-way up the stairs but paused and retraced his steps.

'There is no God,' he said.

'God is nonsense,' Mr Shaffer went on, gesturing vigorously with a folded Yiddish newspaper. 'The rabbis and the rich people talk about God just to keep poor people in their places.' His beaked nose stabbed at us, sombre eyes glowing with passion. 'Don't spend time on such rubbish, children! Learn science, study, think of the future! The world belongs to you, not to God.'

'What a nut!' somebody said when he'd gone.

During supper I told my mother that Mr Shaffer did not believe in God. She cuffed my ears for repeating such blasphemy.

'How is it possible?' she exclaimed, and hurried to tell the neighbours.

The next time I saw Mendel I asked him why his father didn't believe in God. He hunched his shoulders and walked away without answering.

In our neighbourhood, religion was a kind of family affair, to be treated with irony and ambiguity. People made sly jokes about rabbis, and whenever things didn't work out well they addressed asides to the *Rabboine Shel Oilem*, the Lord of the Universe, chiding him for not contriving a better fate for His Chosen People. That is the way of the Jews. Since the time of the Patriarchs they have been on terms of familiarity with Jehovah.

There were also, of course, Anarchists, Communists, Bundists and Socialist Zionists who were outspokenly defiant of the Almighty. They smoked cigarettes on the Sabbath – except in public – and if they went to synagogue at all it was only out of respect for deceased parents, or, because, after all, it was a social occasion. As for fasting on Yom Kippur, the Day of Atonement, they did so because it is good for health to give the stomach a rest once in a while. Sin had nothing to do with it.

In short, for some of our folk in those days God was still father and friend in a hostile world, for others He was merely the opium of the masses. Consequently, the affair of Mendel's soul touched everyone one way or another. There were those who gloated when Susskind, the Hebrew teacher, no longer came to give the boy private tuition; others, when it was learned that lessons were secretly continuing in the teacher's cellar. The score rose for some when Mr Shaffer took his son on a forbidden Sabbath tram ride and was cancelled for others when the grandmother hurried to obtain absolution from the rabbi. She was not one to give up Mendel's soul lightly. At mealtimes, for each blessing Mendel would not speak in the presence of his father, she recited two. As fast as atheistic literature was brought into the house, she carried it down to the dustbin in the yard. In the women's gallery of the synagogue her lamentations rose insistently above the keening of the entire congregation.

Things went from bad to worse. Mr Shaffer and the grandmother ceased talking directly and addressed each other only through the boy. Their lodger, Mr Schulberg, got into the habit of spending his evenings in kosher restaurants meditating gloomily over a glass of lemon tea. As for Mendel himself, there were times when he seemed lonelier than any person I know. He still took pleasure in his father's company, but he loved his grandmother, too, and the strain of remaining loyal to both left a hurt in his eyes for anyone to see. But he was not a boy to talk about such things except, perhaps, to his fiddle which in those days made music of heart-breaking sadness. I think he was genuinely neutral in the struggle that was taking place over his soul. Looking back, I can see that he lived an interior life composed of the intense dreams of solitude, and in the soul of such a person there is room for everything.

It was about this time that the Slutskys moved away to America. They were a family with eight children, nearly all of them girls, and they had been so overcrowded in their two-roomed flat that there were children sleeping all over the place, even under the dining table. Chaim Slutsky had six brothers in Chicago and each of them contributed one hundred dollars to bring the family over. A day after they left Kramer, the furrier, moved into the empty apartment with his wife, two children and spinster sister, Freda.

In as close a community as ours, each newcomer added a new complexity, changing us all a little and sometimes even influencing the whole pattern of our fate. For Mendel Shaffer, the arrival of Kramer's sister, Freda, was momentous. She was a dark, lively woman of twenty-six who sang sentimental songs in a flat, adenoidal voice and laughed through a small opening in her mouth to conceal the loss of her back teeth. Apart from being very short and skinny, she was not bad looking and it was soon observed that Mr Schulberg was paying some attention to her. He had a sly way of watching women, had Mr Schulberg. He would turn his head at an angle away from them and droop his eyelids as if half asleep, but in the narrow slits that remained the swivelled pupils were as sharply focused as binoculars. Still, his interest in Miss Kramer was perplexing for he had never before come close to the objects of his admiration. Every time he saw her he doffed his shabby bowler-hat with an ingratiating smile and held it to his chest like a bouquet of flowers.

Freda seemed flattered, although Mr Schulberg wasn't actually a young, or even middle-aged, man. It might even be that he was trying to sell her a plot in the cemetery. Therefore, her manner remained cool. She didn't even bother to keep her mouth closed when she smiled. Even so, the relationship progressed to the point where they were actually seen in earnest conversation in Mr Schulberg's favourite kosher restaurant. Assuming that he was pleading his suit, people were vaguely scandalized and openly derisive. There must be at least a hundred Yiddish jokes about the mating of old men with young women and at the time they used all of them. Later, when it became clear what Schulberg had really been up to, they had to admit he was not such an old fool, after all.

For following on the restaurant episode the entire Kramer family became ostentatiously friendly to Mendel Shaffer. He rarely managed to pass their threshold without being molested in some way. Mrs Kramer would rush out with a piece of strudel, Freda pierced him with compassionate glances, Mr Kramer offered him as much as sixpence to run some simple errand, and the children urged him to come in and play. All this made Mendel intensely uncomfortable. He tried tiptoeing down the stairs, but was betrayed by his own awkwardness. The Kramers were out like a flash, picked him up, dusted him down and dragged him inside to have iodine dabbed on his grazes. He gave in: what else could he do?

Inevitably, therefore, the day arrived when Mendel's father was lured into the Kramer's apartment in search of his son. Naturally, he had to stay for a glass of tea, dispensed by Freda herself together with some delicious cakes of her own baking. Naturally, also, he could see with his own eyes that the Kramers had a nice family life, eating well and making pleasant company amongst themselves. The atmosphere must have been exceedingly comforting to a lonely man. Mr Kramer wound up the gramophone and played a Russian gypsy melody. It was casually disclosed that although he was related to the famous Sotmarer Rabbis, he'd recently developed some doubts about religion. Perhaps Mr Shaffer had a few ideas on the subject. . . . Splendid! Then why not drop in some evening, drink a little tea and enjoy a good intellectual discussion? Even tomorrow!

So that precious thing, a friendship, was born. After returning from work, Mendel's father would rinse his hands and face at the sink, sit down silently to supper, read the Yiddish paper or listen to Mendel practising his violin. An hour or so later he knocked at the Kramer's door. Freda always opened it to him, smelling of eau-de-cologne and smiling the prim smile that made her seem shyer, and less guileful than she was. The family enveloped him in a warmth as comforting as one of their fur coats. He would talk of religion, politics, hard winters in the Siberian plains, then, reluctantly at first but with growing passion, of Mendel and the way his scheming grandmother sought to make of the boy a hair-splitting Talmudist. The sinewy throat knotted and writhed. Freda Kramer bathed him with the balm of her womanly solicitude. When he returned home to bed misery had abated a little, and soon, no doubt, it began to occur to him how much better it would be if Freda lay in the place now occupied by the gently snoring bulk of Mr Schulberg.

In another corner of the bedroom, behind a sheltering screen that both protected modesty and blocked the draught of the window, the grandmother lay with Mendel cradled in the hollow of her arm. She, too, must have had her thoughts, listening to the creaking of the bed as her son-in-law turned restless in the dark. My mother once told me that if you know how to pray God will make one miracle especially for you. The old woman knew how to pray, but she did not rely on prayer alone.

So time passed and, as you can now guess, a day came when an announcement appeared in the Yiddish newspaper of the forthcoming marriage of Freda Kramer and Mendel Shaffer's father. With some reluctance, Mr Shaffer agreed to a religious ceremony. When he stood under the synagogue canopy, shy and solemn with the gravity of the occasion, beside his eager, diminutive bride, he was clad, like any other Jewish bridegroom, in a black homburg and neatly pressed suit. The ancient, sonorous responses came no differently from his lips than from others.

Marriage is a series of compromises. Freda moved into the Shaffer's apartment and Mr Schulberg moved out. She lit the Sabbath candles and kept a kosher home as meticulously as even the grandmother could wish. A fertile woman, she was frequently pregnant, and with many mouths to feed Mr Shaffer had little time to worry about Mendel's soul. Mendel began to play the fiddle again but couldn't do so often as it might wake the babies. No one cared any longer whether he played it or not. Most people were getting wirelesses in those days and everyone was crazy about dance-band music.

Emanuel Litvinoff

A View from the Seventh Floor

That summer I was sixteen there were no sparrows in the streets, and the sun never shone and the voices of others mocked my despair, laughing ha-ha in the distance. All day I inhaled the hairs of dead foxes, skunks and rabbits in Dorfmann's rat-infested fur workshop, and would do so, it seemed, until my lungs were stuffed full as a feather pillow. At night I slept amid the debris of failure – God had torn up my dreams like an impatient schoolmaster.

In Dorfmann's I was the only one who didn't belong to the family. His wife, the machinist, had big muscular arms and shaved every day, a misfortune she could not conceal by powdering her jaws. Luba, the finisher, an old-fashioned girl, was his niece. Braided plaits of jet-black hair were wound around her delicate ears and her high plump breasts were like two nestling pigeons. She stitched away industriously and blushed when our glances collided. In that place I was her prisoner, thinking of her hotly, with shame, as I stroked the silken pelts spread out on the bench. So even though the pay was meagre and the work hard, I counted these the wages of lust and did not rebel.

'You don't want to improve yourself any more?' my mother said in her suffering voice.

She stood at the stove ladling soup into my plate, the latest baby squirming in the crook of her arm. A man's cardigan hung shapelessly on her body, but her belly was seen to be big again. We were ten already, the largest family in the buildings, and nothing helped, not whispered conferences with neighbours, nor the tubes and syringes concealed among the underwear at the bottom of the wardrobe, and certainly not Fat Yetta, who sometimes lifted the curse of fertility from other women but only left my mother haggard with pain and exhaustion.

'Manny,' she said, 'I'm talking to you!'

My hands reeked of the corpses of small animals and there was no redemption. 'Leave me alone,' I cried. 'I don't want to improve myself.'

'Boobele, take a little soup, it's good for you,' she crooned, forcing the spoon into little Frankie's reluctant mouth. 'And Jacky, stop playing with the sewing machine! Where's Davey! Where's Sonia! Close the door, somebody, there's a terrible draught!' She would have gathered us back into the womb had God's Housing Inspector permitted such overcrowding.

Solly, my stepfather, had the gift of detachment. He stirred his vermicelli soup and read the *Freethinker* with the credulous fascination of a believer. My brothers came in one by one to quarrel, eat ravenously, and depart unsatisfied. Food could not appease our hunger.

'God made the world in six days, but who made God?' Solly said with a dry chuckle.

'Better to think of shoes for the kinder,' my mother replied sombrely. She turned back to me. 'Maybe in night-school you could learn to be a typewriter.'

'Don't speak like a Peruvian,' Solly said. 'You're wasting your breath. That boy's got no ambition, can't you see?'

My ears began to pound like kettle-drums. Tyrants would tremble if they knew my power. I'd blow up banks and start a revolution, invent a miracle, make Rothschild look a pauper. A thousand years would remember my name. I was a bomb waiting to explode the world . . .

'I'll join the army!' I said in a choking voice. 'I'll go to Australia! Maybe I'll be an all-in-wrestler.'

'With your physique?' Solly said. 'Don't make me laugh!'

He laughed. I poured my soup into the sink. Solly rolled up the *Freethinker* and chased me out of the house. That night I didn't go home at all. I hung around in the shadow of a factory doorway until darkness annihilated the street, then slouched to Westminster Bridge and sent my spit flying into the royal Thames.

After thinking it over carefully, I asked Dorfmann for a rise.

'You gone out of your head?' he demanded indignantly. 'With me you got a future, a golden future. For why should you spoil it? In the middle of the busy!' His breath stank of herring and Turkish cigarettes and when I looked away he mistook it for insolence. 'Pay a little respect!' he shouted. Luba came by carrying an armful of furs and brushed against me, weakening my resolution. 'I've got to improve myself!' I insisted doggedly.

He went to confer with Mrs Dorfmann. She turned her bearded face and gazed balefully in my direction, then began to talk back at her husband, beating the air with her hands until he cringed. Dorfmann nodded subserviently and came back. 'Money we don't give for nothing,' he shrugged, his mouth twisted as if by a lemon. 'You work hard another month, maybe yes.' His wife nodded severely from across the room. All that day she tried to catch me slacking. 'Max! The boy! Look at him, the dreamer! Give him something to do!' she said, heaving herself off the machine-stool and plodding on thick legs to the toilet. Dorfmann went out to discuss business over a glass of tea with a skin merchant. I was left alone with Luba. It was so quiet, you could hear the scrape of the needle on her metal thimble.

'What do you do on week-ends?' I stammered.

'On Saturday,' she whispered, without lifting her head, 'I go to the synagogue with my aunt.'

Soft black hair curled on the nape of her slender neck and I was tormented by her narrow, sleepy Russian eyes. I wanted to say something miraculous and unforgettable, or so sharp, cruel and eloquent it would remain a fresh wound all of her life. But instead I said: 'Does your aunt shave on Shabbos?'

I looked at her horrified. She stared back in disbelief.

'Well, it's against the religion, isn't it?' I blustered just as Mrs Dorfmann returned. 'What's going on?' she said sharply. I was already half-way to the door.

The street was full of furriers. There was a sign on Bloom's in the next building. 'Cutters, Nailers, Machinists Wanted,' it said. Mr Bloom was a small brisk man who talked very fast.

'What did Dorfmann pay you?' he demanded.

'I had a future with Dorfmann. He paid me thirty bob.'

Mr Bloom cackled. 'A future? With that shmock? He'll be bankrupt before next season. Do yourself a favour! Here, we got scientific methods – powered machines, refrigeration, the lot. I'll put you on piece-work. As good as being your own master. You can take home two-three pound every week.'

I accepted, of course. There was a pain in my chest as if a lump of living flesh had been torn from me and I wished I was eighteen already, and there was a war. In those days I had the shadowy premonition that unless my life was shattered to pieces and I could put it together differently, I'd never, never be myself.

Working in Bloom's cauterized these raw feelings. Everyone was on piece-work and they grudged time lost on factory gossip and laughter. The machines purred like metal cats; great piles of skins were hurled on cutters' benches, to be stretched, matched and sliced under the quick knives. Wilting in the heat of the great coke ovens, I hammered nails until my fingers blistered. Dinner times, I climbed on to the flat roof above the sixth floor to eat my sandwiches. I leaned against the brick coping with torpid indifference as chimney stacks discharged dense clouds of smoke and poisoned the city. I went to the cinema as often as I could. It was the era of Mae West and, slumped in the masturbating dark, I longed hopelessly for a love that would be both sacred and profane. At home, everybody was squabbling. The infants crawled about the floor and pestered my mother at her dressmaking. My stepfather would come back from work, sleep for a while, then make himself debonair for a night at the dog track. Hurricanes of rage would blow up suddenly and sweep through us all. The house resounded with threats and defiance; plates were thrown, doors were slammed, screams thrilled the neighbours. But there was only inward bleeding, and that was too common to make more than a routine drama.

No, Mr Bloom was wrong. I had done myself no favour at all. What good was the money I was making anyway? I bought a few things – a Japanese cigarette case, a racing saddle for my bike, some steel chest expanders, a six-bladed pocket knife. On my sixteenth birthday, rattling shillings in my pocket, I went with big-nosed Izzy Birnbaum to a temperance dance in Hoxton hoping to find a couple of older girls with experience enough to be more than friendly. Of course, nothing came of that and we ended up drinking bitter beer somewhere, pretending not to care.

More often I used to hang around near Spitalfields Market, where Luba lived with the Dorfmanns, scrutinizing the small windows of their tenement in the hope of seeing her shadow on a curtain. Time passed with excruciating slowness. People stared out at the street, or moved aimlessly in drab over-stuffed rooms, their mouths opening or closing as if gasping for air. Sometimes I saw, or thought I saw, the grapplings of lust, and once a man was brought out on a stretcher with his throat cut. The main diversion came when pubs closed, especially on Saturday nights when professional strong-men and other motley performers were drawn away from their West End pitches by tipsy Cockney generosity.

The one place I never looked for Luba was on the factory roof, but that was where I saw her. It was hot enough to fry a bug and people crowded on top of the buildings as if the Lord Mayor's Show was about to begin at any minute. Workers lay around with unbuttoned shirts playing cards, or luring pigeons on to their shoulders with crumbs. A crowd of men at a window across the street whistled shrilly. I glanced up and there she was on Dorfmann's roof, just a few feet off. We stared at one another, then looked away quickly.

There was a gust of hot wind and a sheet of somebody's newspaper took off, swooping over the chimneys like a clumsy bird. Luba arched her soft-skinned throat to watch it soar towards the dome of St Paul's, and I watched her. We both laughed. Some workmen began to chaff her coarsely. She blushed and edged towards the concealment of a chimney stack. Seizing the excuse for chivalry, I climbed the iron railing, gazed dizzily into the pit of the street sixty feet below, and leaped across. The men set up an ironic cheer.

'I hope my uncle doesn't see you,' Luba said discouragingly. 'He thinks you're a Communist.'

In those days there were still people who believed Bolsheviks ate babies and Soviet girls belonged to everybody, like the means of production. But I'd been expelled from the Young Communist League because, in common with Trotsky, I was against the Russians keeping the Revolution all to themselves. My mother's family had starved to death in the Ukraine and when I mentioned it to a Communist I knew, named Mickey Lerner, he told me you couldn't make an omelette without breaking eggs. I was against making an omelette with people, so I was no longer a Communist, only a Revolutionary.

When I explained all this to Luba, her soft mouth trembled and she sighed with that rich Jewish sadness that is easily aroused at the mention of tragedy. It brought us closer to one another. Her glowing dark eyes and full soft bosom belonged to me a little by reason of that kinship.

'I thought you were an idealist when I first saw you,' Luba said intensely.

The sun blazed up and lit the world from here to China.

She was there again the next day, and the next. It became our routine. As soon as she appeared I climbed over the railings and we sat together, sharing our sandwiches. It was amazing how quickly we felt at ease with one another. Once she asked abruptly: 'Do you believe in God?'

'In God?' I laughed, not because I was amused but because we were there, together, far away from everything.

'Don't laugh,' she said gravely.

Thinking about it for a moment, I had to give God the benefit of the doubt.

'Then how can you believe in the Revolution?' Luba said.

'God believes in the Revolution,' I said.

She told me she was born in the Russian town of Podolsk and was brought to England when her mother died. She would like to be a singer and hummed Yiddish songs remembered from childhood in a sweet, thin voice that trembled with shyness. When I spoke facetiously of the Dorfmanns, she was upset because they were good people and she loved them. I was not to make fun of her aunt's beard. Mrs Dorfmann had been a beautiful girl, but at fifteen she was attacked in a pogrom. Not only did the hair then grow where it shouldn't, but it stopped her aunt from having children, and that was why she could never be a happy woman.

We talked about other people with the grave sympathy of those who feel themselves immune from misfortune. The only trouble was, Luba wouldn't agree to meet me after work because her uncle was very strict. I wanted more time. It wasn't enough, this brief interlude in the middle of the day when the machines fell silent for an hour and we came together under the open eye of the sky.

I hadn't time enough to tell her a hundredth part of my raw yearnings, and I believe Luba felt the same. Her mouth was moist and full; a sad sensuality smouldered in her indolent brown eyes as we talked of going to the country for the day, of visits we would make to the cinema, of rowing boats on the Serpentine and river steamers floating at night past the lighted city.

Birds flying from roof to street and back again gave me

an idea. Hazardously, I said: 'We could meet here after work?'

'On the roof?'

'Yes . . . we'd be all alone.'

The idea amused and embarrassed her. 'They'd send the fire engine to bring us down,' she said.

'Let's try it and see what happens.'

Luba didn't know: she wasn't sure; supposing her aunt should see her? Eventually, however, she came to an adventurous resolve. When the Dorfmann's left she'd make an excuse to go home separately and slip upstairs. But only for a few minutes. A few minutes could be prolonged for an hour, perhaps more. Darkness and silence would rise out of the deserted factories, stars would hang in clusters above our heads, and our pale faces would meet and kiss.

That afternoon I tried to kill time with work, hammering nails into the furs as if each moment was made of metal. The clock on the workshop wall was frozen for hours on end. Then machines ground to a stop, benches were cleared and everyone began to leave. It was six o'clock. I climbed out of the catacombs. At the level of the seventh floor, London was a ghost city at this time. I stood alone among the petrified chimneys, watching the gold medallion of the sun and waiting for Luba.

Footsteps climbed the iron rungs of the skylight. I turned eagerly. Dorfmann's tousled grey head emerged and he stared at me, eyes red-rimmed with fatigue.

'Nu, you didn't expect it would be me?' he said in a sunken voice. 'Low-life! Cumminist! Hasking a young gel to come up on the roof.' He began to screech. 'It's dangerous! You want to break your own neck? Please! It's a free country . . .'

I arrived home to find my brother Abie in a nasty temper. 'Where's my shirt?' he demanded. 'You took my shirt!' I'd dressed myself up in the morning to look decent and it was the only clean shirt my size in the drawer. We started to fight. My stepfather tried to separate us and my mother screamed at us all. The younger boys complained that they couldn't do their homework in all the noise. It was a fairly normal evening. After supper I went out. The moon rode in an empty sky. It looked down at the street as if it was a stranger.

Emanuel Litvinoff

Life Class

The day Chancellor Dollfus was shot in Vienna Morry Spitzer and I joined the art class of the Bethnal Green Men's Institute. I wrote it down in a diary I was keeping at the time. '25 July. Started to do Art. Modelled an egg in clay. The ovoid (egg) is life's basic form – Mr Snood. Death came to pocket Dictator Dollfus today. *Blut fascisti.* Capitalism cannot survive its own contradictions.' I wasn't sure at the time that I'd survive my own contradictions.

I began the diary in a mood of despair. Life was slipping out of my hands. It had to be trapped, somehow, held down. I prowled along Whitechapel Road staring at wax dummies simpering in shop windows; drifted westward with the tide of the city to be washed up at Speakers Corner where men with virulent eyes spoke of the shipwreck of damnation; in Soho alleyways, stirred by a lonely thrill, I watched loitering women through narrowed eyelids, or turned aside to study tracts outside the Church of Christ, Scientist. Nothing entered, neither good nor evil. All around life in its abundance was happening to everybody. I had to make it happen to me.

Morry Spitzer, my best friend at the time, a shy, left-handed boy to whom the world was the wrong way round, was masturbating too much and yearning his spare time away in the front row at the pictures. He worked in his father's kosher butcher-shop disembowelling chickens, although the trade disgusted him so much Morry concealed meat in his pockets rather than eat it and sometimes forgot to get rid of it before it began to stink. During this time, he was intensely absent-minded and was taking a course in Pelmanism to improve his memory. But he couldn't remember to keep himself clean. His shirt was stained with chicken blood, dried spunk encrusted the front of his trousers and he never shaved the tufts of hair that were appearing on his otherwise smooth cheeks.

We were drawn together because we hated the same things and were depressed by our inadequacies. We hated our fathers first, most people afterwards. We were attracted and disgusted by the sexuality of women, and Morry had a vegetarian horror of their flesh. The stilted way they walked on their steep heels reminded him of hens lifting their feet in a farmyard. He was more passive than me. Where he was a reformer according others the grace of improvement, I was a scornful and avenging angel pronouncing the great guilty of corruption, the low of servility. Sometimes I raged to know the secrets of the world the better to destroy it before it reached out and crushed my life – through war, poverty, toil or neglect. And time was short. By eighteen, which seemed the crucial threshold, I aimed to master Karl Marx, become a powerful writer and arm myself with other intellectual weapons of superiority.

Because of this I was impatient with the teaching methods of Mr Snood. He had us sharpening pencils and drawing cubes, cylinders, circles and dead things like Woolworth vases. 'First learn the alphabet, my lads,' he said, 'and in time you'll work up to the poetry of the yuman figure,' pointing at a bench littered with plaster torsos. He talked in this condescending way as if to imply that teaching in Bethnal Green was his form of social service, but I'd seen him sitting alone in the eel-and-pie shop, rolled middle-class umbrella laid across his striped knees, eating a sixpenny sheep's head as if it was the first dinner he'd had in a week.

There were about twelve of us in his class. The two most advanced were a corporation dustman, Arthur Judd, who did water colours of ships lying in palm-fringed lagoons, and an elderly Jew named Miskin, a grocer by trade, old-fashioned enough never to be seen without his skull-cap. He stood in a reflective trance at the easel, smears of paint matting his grey beard, crowding the canvas with monstrously pregnant women, shy and stricken children, rabbis with the angularity of scarecrows brandishing torahs in the face of God. I used to hang around watching him work. He mixed colours so sweet and strong you felt you wanted to lick them, then applied his brush slowly, a stroke here, a touch there, and one face after another flared out as if picked from the darkness by a fire's reflection.

'Would you teach me to paint, Mr Miskin?' I asked him once. He responded with a lop-sided smile. 'If I should split your head, God forbid, I couldn't teach you what you can see mit your own eyes.'

The more I used my eyes, the less I could fit the world together. Take the street we lived in, disorderly with light, colour, texture, voice, posture, movement, noise and silence. We jostled in that brick gulley as if we knew where we were going, but in the verminous night our lungs sucked at the used air as we struggled in a collective dream of suffocation. Panic pursued me behind closed doors. I stood in front of the mirror at home and interrogated my reflection. It was ill put together, the left side's innocence and the right hand's cunning. An abrupt resentful face shaped by an ancestry of misfortune: it looked back at me with disfavour. And behind us both, as daylight withdrew from the room, a shadow brushed the future with its wings.

After a few weeks, Mr Snood decided that we were ready for the human figure. He took down a clay model from a shelf and blew a cloud of dust from its scarred terra cotta body. It's nose was chipped and a crack ran through its left breast. 'The female nood,' he announced, placing it reverently on a plinth. 'You can spend a lifetime studying the female nood.' He was working on a project of his own, a clay bust of a girl with jutting lips like something by Epstein, and periodically stepped back to examine it with pursed approval. Finally, he came and glanced over our shoulders. Morry's drawing was going well, but Mr Snood took a pencil and made swift corrections to mine. 'You've got the proportions of the 'ead wrong, lad. An eighth of the body. Don't give 'er water on the brain.' I showed it to Miskin when it was finished. He scratched the bony bridge of his nose and sighed. 'In Odessa,' he said, 'a boy can catch a sea fish mit a piece of string. A live fish, it moves beautiful.' He handed the drawing back with a deprecating smile. I tore the damned thing up and threw it in the rubbish bin.

There is an entry in my diary dated 10 September. 'Drew another lousy piece of plaster. Felt like smashing it up. It's dead, dead, dead.' I was so obsessed with the idea of studying life at first-hand that I even conceived, and abandoned, the impractical idea of drilling a hole in our bedroom wall to watch Rita Schomberg when she got undressed. Rita was a fat girl of nineteen who wore tight sweaters and looked at me with sleepy concupiscence. She tormented my dreams but wasn't my type at all and I'd only study her naked in the interests of art. Hours on my knees peering through the keyhole as my mother fitted dresses on her customers gave me odd glimpses of female anatomy – broad bloomered bottoms, strapped thighs, flesh bulging over boned corsets. They came together to make a composite Rita Schomberg grotesquely armoured for sex, but I could not find in them the true lineaments of woman, that slim yet voluptuous ideal that drew the leaping tides of lust.

I stood and watched Morry at work in the cubbyhole behind his father's shop. Sawdust and blood were sprinkled over the floor and there were feathers in his hair. He seized a bird, chopped its feet off at the knees and severed its neck with a swift blow of the axe. With bitterness and loathing, he threw the cock's head into a metal bin, then, ripping its scrotum with his forefinger, thrust his hand into the cock's body and pulled out a mass of steaming intestines. The warm mucous smell made me turn aside with nausea. Dead chickens, pierced through the throat, hung in rows on metal hooks. Morry rinsed his hands perfunctorily under the tap and we went off to the pictures.

One Sunday morning that autumn, we trailed two laughing girls in Victoria Park. They sat on a bench by the lake, rubbed their mouths with lipstick and looked at us in their tiny mirrors. One girl lifted her leg and slowly crossed her knees. Morry dug his hands deeply into his pocket and caught his lower lip between his teeth. He stared sadly and vacantly at the muddy green water.

'Did you notice that movement?' he said in a hoarse voice. 'She's got good legs,' I replied miserably. 'They swell up nice at the top.'

We shivered and became silent. The girl twisted her slender ankle, glanced at her friend and spoke in an undertone. They both laughed. I imagined more than I saw – thigh muscles joining the strong resilient buttocks and the groin, dark, tender and voracious as a Negro's mouth.

The girls departed as swiftly as migrant birds, leaving the park desolate. Brown leaves drifted over the surface of the lake. I ached like a bereaved bridegroom.

At the end of term, Mr Snood made an announcement. Two pictures by Arthur Judd were exhibited with distinction in the annual display of works by Local Government Officers. His own *Jeune Femme*, which no doubt we'd all watched him model with profit, had been purchased by a private collector. Of the younger students, he particularly wished to congratulate Morris Spitzer for his grasp of proportion, without which there could never be True Beauty.

'This class is ready for the yuman figure, the nood,' Mr Snood stated solemnly. His eyes shifted under our collective stare. 'The living nood,' he added quietly and impressively.

Morry and I exchanged a flushed and earnest glance. I scarcely heard as Mr Snood went on to warn us we must merit the faith in us shown by the Bethnal Green Men's Institute, cast out all dirty thoughts and approach the living nude with fitting reverence. A dazzling image of Rita Schomberg plump and naked on a plinth had appeared in the centre of my mind and set off embarrassing physical reactions. In those days I was almost always tumescent. A poem, the lonely reflection of street-lamps on wet pavements, unexpected news, saxophones, even a barrow high and aromatic with fruit, any of these could give me an unbearable erection.

We arrived early on the first day of the new term, but were not the earliest. About sixty men of all ages crowded the classroom. I recognized some as members of the Rabbit Breeders' Club and several elderly tailors from the English for Foreigners class. Mr Snood distributed sheets of cartridge paper and pencils with brisk excitement and everyone jostled for a place near the front. At the rear of the room, wearing an aloof constabulary expression, was the Principal. Mr Snood conferred with him for what seemed a very long time. We began to feel that something was not quite right. Where was the model? She could only be in the small adjoining office where the teacher did his paper work and from which she must eventually make her astonishing appearance.

Mr Snood went fussily to the door, opened it, inserted his head and called: 'We're ready if you are.'

A figure emerged wrapped in a bath robe and made its stately progress down the studio. There was heavy breathing followed by a collective groan. I still remember the shock; we'd been conned. The model wasn't even female. It was a ladies' hairdresser named Arnold, well-known in the Bethnal Green Road as a tim-tum, a person of indeterminate sex, because of his mincing walk, his wrist bracelet, and the tight seat of his trousers.

Arnold gave us a courtly nod and disrobed without hesitation. His genitals sagged limply below his hairy belly. I think we'd have been less embarrassed if he had been a woman. Nobody had ever seemed so naked. So unsightly a body should never have been exposed undressed to strangers. One by one men began to sneak out of the room. The Principal left after clearing his throat noisily. Mr Miskin went back to painting the picture in his head. I drew Arnold with the heroic proportions of a heavyweight champion as if somehow, obscurely, this mitigated the disaster.

It was after this that Morry and I decided we'd set up our own studio. The problem was where. He shared a bedroom with his fifteen-year-old sister and an unmarried aunt. In my own family you even had to fight for a corner of the kitchen table. Space was the ultimate luxury. There was a derelict cellar under Morry's shop, too damp for human habitation and less romantic than a poor artist's attic, but it was something and one Sunday morning we started to clear the place out.

In those days nobody threw anything away that could be patched, cannibalized or traded for a piece of china. Morry's cellar was a warehouse of such articles. There were mildewed boots with splayed uppers, stinking mattresses, empty bottles, upholstery stuffing, rags, splintered glass, a broken w.c. and other abject refuse. Luxuriant green mould had grown over a dilapidated leather sofa and when it was moved we found the decayed corpse of a cat, its tiny yellow teeth were bared in a grimace of terror. It must have been dead a long time. Dark came before the mess was all shifted, leaving a space about ten feet square. A pauper's ration of moonlight filtered through the metal grating in the pavement. It would never be much lighter. Even a millionaire couldn't have brought the sky down to a cellar like that. But it was a place from which to climb. It was a beginning. We were ready to start.

At this stage I ought to explain about Morry's aunt. She was a handsome, bitter woman of twenty-eight, who'd had a love affair with a man in a dry-cleaning business in Brick Lane. He'd disappeared suddenly and it turned out he had a wife in Poland. As far as people in the neighbourhood were concerned Morry's aunt was henceforth a soiled woman. At best she could only look forward to marriage with an elderly widower. There were ugly rumours that Morry's father only kept her in the house because she was loose, and she walked around the streets with a cold implacable fury as if daring some busybody to say these things aloud so that she might tear the slanderous tongue out of their heads – man or woman. Morry was terribly afraid of this aunt. She was angry about everything he did. When he slept she searched his pockets and became even more furious for, of course, there was nothing to find – only packets of Woodbines, or loose change, or bits of meat he'd forgotten to throw away. He was afraid she'd come snooping into the cellar when we were there and catch us without clothes, because we intended to pose for one another, of course.

But it didn't deter us. All our beginning used to be optimistic. We bought sticks of charcoal and new blocks of drawing paper and prepared to write a fresh chapter into our lives that grey Sunday morning the studio was inaugurated. It was now early winter. The November sky slid over the streets like an iron shutter. I arrived shivering with cold and excitement to find Morry tiptoeing around the cellar arranging things. 'Shush!' he cautioned me. 'They're all still asleep.' He'd smuggled in a couple of kitchen chairs and fixed a carbon mantle on the disused gas-jet. It gave off a warm and comfortable glow. We grinned at one another with delight and, undressing quickly down to his jock-strap, Morry dropped to one knee and adopted an athletic pose.

We'd never imagined any place could be so cold as that cellar. The gas-light created only an illusion of cosiness. After twenty minutes Morry couldn't stop his teeth chattering and kept jumping up to slap his arms against his sides. I wasn't looking forward to my turn at all. When it came we were both getting a bit irritable. I sat numbly on the edge of the chair, my forehead propped up by a clenched fist, trying to hold the naked soles of my feet away from the icy concrete floor.

'What are you supposed to be?' Morry said, studying my pose from all angles.

'What do I look like? Jesus Christ?'

'You look as though you're having a crap.'

'If you know your Greek sculpture,' I replied cuttingly, 'you'll recognize Rodin's *Thinker*.'

He started to laugh and I was furious. Soon we were jumping about and pummelling one another, hilarious as a couple of maniacs.

Morry's father appeared, slippered and unshaven, a woollen nightcap on his polished bald head, and stared in astonishment. I put my trousers on as the old man carefully looked away. 'Boychik, boychik,' he grumbled reproachfully to Morry. 'Fighting in the cellar, like a drunken goy!'

For a couple of weeks we didn't meet. Bad things were happening in Europe. People were on the move trundling bundles in prams, and frontier guards played football with stateless Jews in the no-man's-land between Germany and Poland. Night after night I scuffled with Mosley's fascists while Morry, who shirked violence, humped his loneliness into back-street cinemas. I saw him once when I was walking down Brick Lane. He was eating chips out of a newspaper, staring dejectedly at girls' legs. It looked as if he'd mislaid himself somewhere and was wandering around with little hope of finding himself again. 'Hey, Morry!' I called. 'I'll come over to do some sketching on Sunday.' He turned, blinking vaguely.

'All right, I'll expect you,' he said in an embarrassed voice. 'Going to a meeting?'

'Sure. Wanna come?'

His eyes had the fixed stunned look that came from sitting close up to the screen in smoky darkness at the Pavilion. I hurried away to join my boisterous guerrillas in another skirmish.

On Sunday the weather had changed and a bright winter sun made it seem pointless to spend the morning in a dingy cellar. By the time I came Morry's family were already up and about. We could hear his father overhead scrubbing the bloodstained block on which he hacked and butchered his carcases. Standing naked in the striped light that came through the cellar grating, I thought of the cold sun above

Poland's frontier. Miskin's black rabbi stared at his God with slaughtered eyes. Oh, to be Lenin commanding the Revolution with an uplifted finger; Budyenny speaking a terse soldierly message as his Red Cavalry galloped into the white Siberian desert. *Blut fascisti.*

'Would you fight against Hitler, Morry?' I said. 'Even if it was a capitalist war?'

He extended his pencil and measured my physical proportions with one eye. 'I'm a pacifist,' he replied. 'You know that.' He made some swift alterations to his sketch and showed it to me. There was a thrusting masculinity in the drawing. Thighs, shoulders and neck strained against an invisible obstacle and the penis was as supple and dangerous as a serpent's head.

'It's good,' I said.

The compliment pleased and embarrassed him. 'You really think so? Really?' He hurried out to pin it up in his bedroom.

I stood by the window smoking a cigarette when the door reopened. It was Morry's aunt. For a moment we stared at each other in petrified silence, then she half-turned distractedly and said: 'Oh, it's you! I'm sorry.' As I reached out stealthily for my clothes she appraised me with a direct, severe, yet passionate gaze. Her bosom strained against the cloth of her dress. My skin burned and I doubled up sharply to conceal my embarrassing erection, but she did not take her eyes off me for a moment. In that instant I knew that all the stories about her were lies. She had the sadness of small Jewish towns hemmed in by ancient curses, and she was afraid of me. It was as if I was twenty-one already and master of half the world. I stood up slowly and began to dress, not even pausing when she left the cellar and quietly closed the door.

Something happened to me about that time. Suddenly I wrote a poem. The words came to me unexpectedly one day during dinner-break at work. I found a crumpled piece of paper in my pocket and wrote them down. 'Farewell O

Queen of the Night, dark mistress of my cosmic dreams.' It was a strange thing to write and I wondered what it meant. But if I failed to understand how the words came, I knew with extraordinary elation that they were a message from inner space. Things would never be the same again.

Biographical Notes

John Updike

born in Shillington, Pennsylvania in 1932 and educated there, at Harvard and at the Ruskin School of Fine Art, Oxford, where he spent a year on a Knox fellowship. His novels to date are *The Poorhouse Fair, The Centaur, Rabbit, Run, Of the Farm,* and *Couples.* His volumes of short stories include *Pigeon Feathers, The Music School,* and *The Same Door.* He has published three books of poetry, *The Carpentered Hen, Telephone Poles,* and *Midpoint,* a book of literary essays, and numerous contributions to the *New Yorker.* He and his wife live in Ipswich, Massachusetts, with their four children and have recently spent nine months in England.

Sylvia Plath

born in Boston, Massachusetts, in 1932, she took her degree at Smith College. While on a Fulbright Scholarship to Newnham College, Cambridge, she met the poet Ted Hughes, whom she married in 1956. They spent two years in the United States where a tattoo artist, encountered in Boston, inspired 'The Fifteen Dollar Eagle'. She returned to England, living first in London, where her daughter was born, and later in Devonshire where she had a son. She died in London in 1963. She wrote two volumes of poetry *The Colossus* and *Ariel* (published posthumously) and a novel, *The Bell Jar.*

Emanuel Litvinoff

born in the East End of London in 1915. He has been war poet (*The Untried Soldier*; *A Crown for Cain*), novelist (*The Lost European*; *The Man Next Door*), and is currently writing plays for television (ten in the last three years). The stories published here are from a series of semi-autobiographical sketches about growing up in the East End between the wars which will be collected in sequence into a volume to be entitled *Journey through a Small Planet*.

Also by John Updike

The Same Door

In these seventeen crystalline stories John Updike takes ordinary situations – a teenager trying to impress his girl friend . . . a man in a rush-hour bus attracted by two beautiful women, one a blonde, the other a Negress . . . a Greenwich Village dinner party for three . . . two old college buddies' reunion . . . marital in-fighting . . . and makes you feel involved, in the aggression, the lust and the bitterness; in the frustration and the agony, say of old-age drawn to youth, or in the sadness of a botched job or a withered friendship. John Updike makes you, as one reviewer put it, quiver to be alive.

Couples

The Music School

Of the Farm

The Poorhouse Fair

The Centaur

Pigeon Feathers and Other Stories

Rabbit, Run

Assorted Prose

Some of Sylvia Plath's poetry is printed in

The New Poetry

Edited by A. Alvarez